A Christmas Staged for Love

LaCharmine (L.A.) Jefferson

Published by SQS Publishing, 2023.

A CHRISTMAS STAGED FOR LOVE

First edition. December 16, 2023.

Copyright © 2023 LaCharmine (L.A.) Jefferson.

ISBN: 979-8991001106

Written by LaCharmine (L.A.) Jefferson.

This book is dedicated to widows learning to love again.

Act 1

Scene 1

The Monday after Thanksgiving, Melissa braced herself against the biting wind as she headed to her happy place, Rose Garden Senior Living. It was the closest thing she had to a baby. Since opening its doors to the first residents three years prior, she found herself looking forward to being there more than being at her own home.

With the official start of the Christmas season, for the first time in two years, she was genuinely excited about the holiday festivities. Not the festivities at home, but the ones at "The Garden", her affectionate nickname for the center.

It was 8:30 a.m., half an hour earlier than her usual arrival time, but she wanted to get a head start on the day. Her schedule was packed. Zoom meetings with the health department officials, followed by meetings with her staff regarding those meetings. Then she would be welcoming a new resident to the facility, and, hopefully, concluding interviews for the much-needed activity coordinator.

Thanks to the Covid-19 pandemic of 2020, good employees were hard to come by and even harder to keep. If the world didn't learn anything else during the unexpected health crisis, it was that people could start lucrative businesses and work on their own time. They have more work/life balance than any company could give them. While that was great for them, it left business owners like her in a pinch trying to keep her establishment running smoothly. She didn't have any work-from-home or come-to-work-when-you-feel-like-it positions. Her business —caring for the needs of one of society's most vulnerable populations-seniors—required hands on employees.

With the first part of her day heavy in administrative tasks, she looked forward to decorating the center and putting up the Christmas tree with her staff and finally meeting the new resident, Paul Walker. She and his daughter, Felicia, had had several pleasant conversations over the past few weeks. Melissa was looking forward to meeting her, too.

As owner and director of the center, she did not have to be hands-on with everything that happened at the center. But she enjoyed every part of it. Participating in big and small aspects of the center's operations was her way of adding her personal touch. She was sure that was why her staff and residents interacted so well with each other. Her heart swelled with pride whenever she thought of the pleasant working and living environment she helped to create for jeeryone.

"Good morning, Ms. Fields. How are you this morning?" Mr. Binion, the building security officer, greeted her, holding the door open.

"Thank you," Melissa said, smiling in return and handing him the coffee she had picked up from the coffee shop down the street.

"And this is for you. Dark roast, black, one sugar. Just like you like it, right?"

"Oh wow. Thank you, Ms. Fields. You really know how to make a guy feel special. You're going to make a man a great wife someday."

She nearly lost her footing in her low-heeled, tall. black leather boots. A kind, mannerly older man, she knew Mr. Binion meant no harm. He had been working at Rose Garden for only a year and had no way of knowing that she had already been a great wife to Maurice, who had died prematurely due to a rare lung disease diagnosed too late.

She and Maurice had eventually found their way back to each other after ending their relationship when they went to separate colleges. He went south to an HBCU, while she stayed close to home in Michigan, after her parents' divorce. Her mother was devastated. Melissa could not bear to leave her. She and Maurice thought they would reunite soon after, but life had other plans for them. Maurice joined the fraternity his father belonged to and immersed himself in that life, eventually dating and marrying a sorority girl.

Melissa was crushed at the news. She considered Maurice to be her soulmate. It took her a few years to stop comparing every guy she dated to Maurice. They never measured up. Eventually, she settled for a decent guy, Derrick. He was an investment banker who was head over heels in love with her. After two years of dating, he proposed. At 28 years old, she was tempted to say yes, to escape the feeling of being in limbo.

Maybe becoming a wife, starting a family, would help. But her conscience wouldn't let her. She had never aspired to be just anyone's wife; she wanted to be Maurice's wife.

Five years later, Maurice privately messaged her on Facebook. He was coming for a visit during Christmas and wanted to see her. Melissa was ecstatic and immediately shared the news with her mother.

"Is his wife coming, too?" Her mother, a fierce protector of her only child's heart, asked just in case Melissa had forgotten that the love of her life had married another woman.

Melissa wanted to see him whether he was married or not. If for nothing else, to see if her heart still palpitated in his presence. Besides, she concluded, maybe if she saw that Maurice was happily married, she would be forced to move on with her life.

Lucky for her, when she and Maurice met up for dinner a week before Christmas, he confessed that he married the wrong woman for the wrong reasons. He divorced two years earlier. He spent the first year gathering himself together and the second mustering the courage to reach out to Melissa.

The rest of the week unfolded into a whirlwind reconciliation, culminating in her and Maurice marrying on Christmas Day. Maurice's fraternity brother, Jerome, already in town for the holiday, stood as his best man, while Melissa's best friend, Alana, supported her. They had an impromptu wedding beside the snow-covered fountain on Belle Isle. Her body shivered from the winter chill, but the fervent love she shared with Maurice radiated from within, providing her with all the warmth she needed. This was undoubtedly the most spontaneous act she had ever committed in her life. But that was the influence Maurice had on her. He was the only person to get her out of her comfort zone and embrace life freely.

Melissa had lost hope of experiencing happiness again, but she did. She lived every day of her life with Maurice in sheer bliss, until God took him away two years later.

"Thanks, Mr. Binion," she said, glancing over her shoulder as she navigated the corner of the entry hallway. She peeked into the community room on her left, where some of her staff and resident volunteers had already started retrieving the Christmas decorations from storage.

"Good morning," she greeted them cheerfully. "Don't start without me," she playfully warned, quickening her pace towards her office.

"Okay," they responded together.

She exchanged greetings with everyone she passed on the brief walk to her office, located at the back of the office suites.

Once in her office, Melissa placed her coffee on the coaster atop her desk. She effortlessly slid the strap of her messenger bag over her head, letting it fall to the floor beside her chair. Then she slowly pulled her arms out of the wool coat she wore and hung it on the vacant hook of the wooden coat hanger in the corner.

With a swift press of the power button, her computer sprung to life, filling the office with a familiar hum. Melissa settled her generous hips into her chair and began pulling out paperwork from her bag. She then indulged in the first sip of her coffee, appreciating its perfect temperature and the well-blended hazelnut and caramel flavors.

She typed her username and password into their proper fields to access her system. The recently upgraded WIFI loaded her desktop in record time. As all the icons materialized on the blue background, she opened her Outlook mail system and clicked on the calendar to confirm the day's activities.

10:30 a.m H.R

12:30-2:00   pm   Contractor   Stroll-One   Source Contracting,

T & J Builders, Top Gun Contracting

4:00 pm New Resident move-in Phillip Walker

She viewed the day ahead as packed yet manageable. There was a small window between her meeting with HR specialist, Deneen, to review candidates for the administrative assistant role—a position to back up Rebecca, who was eight months pregnant and soon going on maternity leave—and the time reserved for general contractors. If the past two Fridays were any indication, where most contractors didn't show up, she might have ample time in her schedule.

Finding a reputable and professional general contractor to build a stage in the community room of Rose Garden had been difficult. She came up with the idea in early spring, thinking there was plenty of time. She was so confident that she had the staff and interested residents start preparing for their first Christmas extravaganza, assuming the stage would be ready by now. But her email and voicemail were filling up with inquiries from residents about whether the stage would be ready in time. She assured them it would be but had no idea that the 2020 pandemic hardship loans and grants that everybody and their mama had received since Covid that all the contractors in her area would be booked. Those available either missed appointments or quoted rates far above her budget. Now, with Christmas a month away, the staff and residents were ready, but without a stage. Melissa hoped that setting aside time on Fridays, her least busy day at the center, for contractors to potentially show up, would ease some of the stress she was feeling.

While she remained hopeful about finding a suitable contractor for the stage, Melissa's enthusiasm peaked at the thought of the last item on her calendar: the arrival of a new resident. She cherished being present during these moments. Understanding the complexities and emotions involved in the decision to move one's parents into a senior home, she recognized that it wasn't always about illness. Sometimes, it was the harsh reality that fear of change brought out in people.

Melissa aimed to make this transition as uncomplicated and enjoyable as possible. She kept an assortment of wines and non-alcoholic beverages ready and routinely ordered fruit trays, sub sandwiches, and a variety of cheese and crackers from Kimmy's Delight Catering. This catering service was a black-owned small business, and its owner's mother resided at Rose Garden, adding a personal connection.

She set an alarm on her phone for 3:30 p.m. to ensure she was ready to greet Felicia and her father, Phillip Walker. Her extensive correspondence with Felicia, through emails and phone calls in preparation for this move, had fostered a sense of deep familiarity, almost as if they were long-time friends.

After spending a few more minutes reviewing her emails for any urgent matters, Melissa stood up, preparing to head to the community room. Just then, Sabrina, one of her staff volunteers, knocked on her office door.

"Ms., uh, Mrs... I'm sorry, Ms. Melissa," Sabrina stumbled, her expression one of slight confusion.

"It's okay, Sabrina. Remember what we discussed last week?" Melissa had always advocated for a familial atmosphere at the Garden, preferring to be addressed by her first name rather than her official title. While most staff adapted quickly, Sabrina, who joined six months ago, found it challenging. At sixty-five, with her hair a mix of salt and pepper, Sabrina struggled to address her boss so informally. Melissa proposed "Ms. Melissa" as a compromise, but even this seemed to be a hurdle for Sabrina.

"Don't worry. I'm going to get it right one day, I promise," Sabrina said respectfully.

Melissa joined her hands in a prayer-like gesture and smiled at Sabrina. "Great. What do you need?"

"Oh yes, I just wanted to let you know that we're nearly finished with the decorations in the community room. So, if you have work that needs your attention here, there's no need to come down."

"That's impossible!!" Melissa exclaimed in a higher-pitched tone than usual. "It looked like you guys were just getting started." She hated to think that her mother was right when she said the staff preferred to do the decoration without her assistance. That would explain why whenever she announced that she put it on her calendar to help with decorations, they would either start sooner than planned or create a reason why they had to change the date altogether. Last year, someone supposedly took the boxes of decorations home by accident. And it happened to be the day before Melissa was going out of town for a conference. Naturally, the decorations were all done when she returned two days later.

She knew that her emotions could be a bit much at this time of the year but that was to be expected. Christmas was already a special time of the year before she married Maurice. But when they reconnected, revived their love in twenty-four hours, and they became husband and wife on Christmas day, the holiday sky-rocketed to her favorite day of the year! And now, three years after losing him, the only way she got through the month was by focusing on bringing joy to those around her. A big part of that was going all out with the decorations at the Garden, where she spent most of her time, gift-giving, holiday parties, and community service. With the world slowly opening back up since the pandemic, Melissa hoped she could get back to filling her evenings and weekends with anything that kept her away from out of her house and focused on others.

Just because she cried a few times one year when hanging the purple ornaments, Maurice's favorite color, didn't mean she should be excluded from the fun. This was the fourth year since Maurice died. She had to be better.

People know they can hold onto stuff, Melissa thought sullenly.

A quick glance down at her Apple watch, she sucked her teeth and looked Sabrina in the eye. "I've only been in my office for twenty minutes. With all the extra decorations that I bought; it should have taken longer than that."

"I guess we were moving faster than usual," Sabrina responded, her gaze darting everywhere in the room except into Melissa's eyes.

"Fine," Melissa acquiesced. She resolved to leave the staff to their tasks without her intervention.

"Okay," she said aloud. Sabrina exhaled a sigh of relief, exiting the office and gently closing the door behind her.

Melissa reached for her cell phone, tapping the Apple Music icon. She navigated to her Christmas playlist, selecting her favorite Jackson 5 Christmas song, *"Christmas Won't Be the Same This Year."* Humming the lyrics under her breath, Melissa felt a poignant truth settle in her heart: Christmas had never been the same again.

Scene 2

PHILIP JR., AFFECTIONATELY known as P.J. to his family and friends, felt a sense of gratification in being able to assist with his father's move to the senior home today. His carpentry business and apprenticeship program kept him extremely occupied, leaving little room to help his sister, Felicia, with their father's recent needs. The influx of multiple stimulus checks and additional unemployment benefits since the pandemic had quadrupled his client list. Without the aid of his apprentices, keeping up with the soaring work demands would have been near impossible.

Felicia, on the other hand, shut down her hair salon at the pandemic's outset. Consequently, she had more time to dedicate to their father, especially after their mother's passing last year. Regardless of her circumstances, Felicia would have made the time; such was her nature as a daughter, sister, and friend. She never voiced her burdens, and it was up to her loved ones to step in and alleviate the pressures she silently shouldered.

Phillip Sr.'s decision to downsize, sell the house, and move into a senior home might have been a way of adapting to a new phase in life. When Felicia broke down in tears hearing this news at dinner with her and P.J., Phillip Sr. tried to console her.

"Don't worry baby girl. Your mother and I saved for this time in our lives. If the Lord hadn't called her home, we would be making this move together," Phillip Sr. said, trying to comfort his emotional daughter.

"But I promised Mom I'd take care of you," Felicia said, tears streaming. "So, I'm failing her too."

P.J. quickly got up and put his hand on his sister's shoulder. "Felicia, stop it. You're too hard on yourself. You're not failing anyone. Dad still needs your help with preparing for the move and finding the right retirement home."

"Right, Dad?" P.J. asked, hoping his parents hadn't already chosen a senior home.

"That's right, baby girl. I still need your help," Phillip Sr. said, his arm around Felicia's other shoulder.

Relieved, P.J. went back to his seat and they resumed their meal. The next day, Felicia started her task of finding the best senior home for their father. Even though P.J. trusted Felicia and their father's decision, she kept him in the loop with every step. They narrowed it down to Rose Garden and Heaven-Sent Senior Living. Felicia chose Rose Garden because it was black- and woman owned, which was important to her as a black woman business owner herself. She also grew to like and respect Ms. Fields, the owner, during the application process.

"Bro, I appreciate you want to handle the move, but I was looking forward to meeting Ms. Fields. We can do the move together," Felicia pleaded with P.J. on move-in day. He had taken the day off work to help with the heavy lifting of the day and provide some relief to his sister. He expected his gesture, including the $100 gift card for Felicia, to be better received.

"Sis, you've done the bulk of everything up to this point. And I'm sure you'll be hanging out with Dad at his new residence every chance you get while I'm working like a mule. Just let me handle this one thing while I can, and you take a day of self-care for yourself. Isn't that what all y'all women talk about these days? Self-care." P.J. said, his full lips curling into a grin.

"Whatever!" She said, punching him lightly on his shoulder. "While you're playing, you're going to need some self-care yourself with all the work you're doing these days. As a matter of fact, you should really be resting since you finally managed to get some days off."

This girl, P.J. thought to himself.

Sometimes he didn't understand why his sister had such a hard time accepting help when offered. She was right, though. He had been working seven days for months. If not on actual customer projects, he was on job sites working with his students. But unlike his sister, when he came home from work, his time was his own. He didn't have anyone that he needed to care for or be emotionally or physically available for so he could handle it. He had no complaints about his life.

"I'm pulling the big brother card. Go home and chill out. I'll let you know when Dad is settled in. Have a good day." He said, opening the door for her to walk through. Felicia looked at him one last time, flipped her hand at him in a "forget you" motion, and walked toward her car.

"You better call me as soon as you're done," she commanded.

As soon as P.J. closed the door, his father appeared at the top of the stairs. "I didn't think that girl would ever leave!" Phillip Sr. said, slapping the top of his leg, bellowing out a hearty belly laugh. "I didn't think I'd ever get my son to myself to get all up in his business. And not that business that pays the bills, either."

P.J. knew what his dad was talking about. It was the only thing he has repeatedly talked about once he was confident that his only son was successful in business and a productive member of society—women. The question was always when was he going to pick one to settle down with.

"What's that, Pops?" P.J. baited.

"You already know," Phillip Sr. started. "What's going on with the ladies? You know your sister told me that even with her shop being closed, she still has clients that call asking her about you. Obviously, there's no shortage of available women. You just need to pick one, get married, and give me a couple more grandkids." Phillip Sr. said, making his way down the stairs, and looking over the boxes of books from his late wife's collection awaiting pickup by the Salvation Army. The three of them pitched in to pack up her clothes six months after she passed away, but he'd wanted to keep the books because they'd brought her so much joy in her final days. But he was okay donating them knowing he couldn't take everything with him to his retirement home. He realized that he didn't need physical things of hers to carry her in his heart every day. He let P.J. and Felicia choose the ones they wanted to keep and boxed everything else up.

Felicia knew better than to tell him about any of her clients calling about him. He respected his sister and her business too much to bring the drama of dating her clients into her workspace. He didn't want to be responsible for Felicia losing clients because they were mad that things didn't work out with her brother. There were too many other avenues for him to meet women when he was ready.

"Pops, I haven't even had time to worry about these ladies. My business is my priority right now." P.J. was single. He enjoyed every bit of his singleness in his twenties and thirties. Having his pick of any woman he wanted, whenever he wanted her. Only a select few managed to motivate him to want to commit long-term, but never marriage. Until he met a woman with the gentle, yet impenetrable and lovingness that he saw in his mother and sister, he didn't see marriage in his future. And now, at forty-three, the pickings of women left him with a feeling of hopelessness. In his business, he met countless attractive women who were extremely accomplished and polished. But either they were too aggressive, eager for a baby if they hadn't had children yet, or they wanted to catapult him to the altar just because they were sexually compatible and enjoyed each other's company. None of that appealed to him.

Phillip Sr laughed out loud! "Well, son, that was all fine and good when you were a young buck, but those gray hairs peeking out of your five o'clock shadow say that those days are behind you. I'd like to have a grandson from my namesake to know the family lineage is continuing."

"I'll see what I can do, Dad. Just don't hold your breath. It's very few women out there with mom's qualities." PJ said.

"Your mother? Oh, boy. That's not what you need to be looking for. Your mother was one of a kind and the last of her generation. You've got to look at the women of today through a different lens."

"You want me to settle?"

"No. I would never suggest that. I know the right woman is out there for you. I bet if you hit up some of these Christmas parties coming up, you can meet your wife and have a baby next year."

"Okay, Dad. Now you're getting beside yourself. I'm not looking for a wife for Christmas. Let's focus on getting these boxes organized. The movers will be arriving shortly.

Scene 3

MELISSA WAS LISTENING rather impatiently to the only contractor who showed up. He was explaining how the prices of material had increased and were in short supply to justify his fifteen-thousand-dollar quote that she knew would have been five thousand less pre-covid. Yes, Melissa wanted to the stage built but she was not willing to pay anything for it. As she said goodbye to the contractor, she was beginning to accept that she would just have to wait for these post-pandemic prices to subside.

Melissa's mood sank a little bit, but the pending arrival of Mr. Walker and his daughter gave her something to look forward to. The vintage white and winter green welcome banner she ordered from Amazon was the perfect addition to the holiday decorations in the lobby. It was the first thing new residents saw when they walked into the building and Melissa was confident it created the warm, family environment she wanted residents to feel they were becoming a part of. She couldn't wait for Mr. Walker and his daughter to arrive in the next ten to fifteen minutes.

She stayed near the lobby to be close by when Mr. Walker and his daughter arrived. While waiting, Melissa was arranging the faux presents under the Christmas tree that the staff had put up earlier that morning.

She quickly made her way to the front desk when she received the call that Mr. Walker had arrived. But, to her surprise, it wasn't Mr. Walker and his daughter waiting in the lobby. Instead, it was Mr. Walker accompanied by a handsome younger version of himself, presumably his son. Melissa was so surprised that she momentarily forgot the usual welcome she extended to all new residents.

"Hello. Are you the director, Mrs. Fields?" the younger man inquired. "We were told a Mrs. Fields would be coming down."

"Oh, yes. Yes, I am," she replied, offering her hand. "Welcome to Rose Garden, where every day feels like waking up in a bed of roses." Realizing her initial startled look, she quickly added, "My apologies. I was expecting Mr. Walker and his daughter, Felicia."

"Oh. Is it okay that I'm here instead? We probably should have informed you about the change in plans beforehand," he said apologetically.

"No, it's fine. I had several conversations with her and was just looking forward to meeting her in person."

"I'm sorry if I've disappointed you," he said with a slight smile.

Melissa, feeling her almond skin flush with embarrassment, quickly corrected the impression she had obviously given. "Oh, goodness! I didn't mean to imply that. Okay," she paused, trying to compose herself. "I'm Ms. Fields, but please call me Melissa. And you are?"

"I'm Phillip Jr, but you can call me PJ," he said, shaking her hand. He noted the softness of her hand just as she quickly withdrew it.

"Well, I guess we should proceed with the move-in," Phillip Sr., the resident, interjected. "The movers just text me that they're pulling up to the loading area."

"Absolutely," Melissa said, excitedly regaining her bearings. "Shall we head up? The movers know exactly where to bring your things."

She guided the gentlemen to the elevator, pointing out important places along the way. These details were mainly for Phillip Jr.'s benefit since Phillip Sr. had already toured the facilities with his daughter a few months earlier.

The three of them rode the elevator to the third floor, enveloped in silence except for the soulful Christmas tunes softly playing through the speakers. Phillip Sr.'s unit was just three doors from the elevators, next door to where Melissa's mother resided.

"Well, here we are, Mr. Walker. Your new humble abode," Melissa announced, unlocking, and opening the door to reveal a spacious two-bedroom, partially furnished apartment.

"Man, I was half expecting to see garland, snowflakes, and ornaments on the walls when you opened the door," the younger Mr. Walker remarked with a curling smile.

"Does that mean you think we've overdone the decorations a bit for the holiday season?" Melissa inquired.

"Maybe just a tad," he replied, pinching his thumb and index finger together slightly.

"A regular ole Mr. Scrooge, I see," Melissa commented.

"I wouldn't go that far," he quipped.

"Well, you should," Phillip Sr. interjected. "I can't recall seeing a Christmas decoration in your house since you bought that huge place."

"Dad, please don't start about the size of my house. It's what I wanted and could afford."

"Mmmhmm, a four-bedroom house for a bachelor. Makes sense only if you plan on filling it."

"Okay, Dad. I doubt Ms. Fields wants to hear you pushing me to find a wife and give you more grandkids." P.J. interjected, just as the movers arrived off the elevator.

"Perfect timing, it seems," Melissa said with an awkward smile. "I'll leave you to it with the movers, then come back to check that you're all settled in."

After one last smile at the Walker men, she left them to handle the move and walked down to her mother's unit a few doors away.

"Hey, Mom. It looks fabulous in here," Melissa called out as she entered the unit, admiring the expert decorations arranged by her mother, Lorraine. Before retiring, Lorraine had built a lucratively successful decorating business alongside her full-time nursing job. Her passion for decorating, particularly for Christmas, had deeply influenced Melissa. They both held themselves to the highest standards in terms of originality, color coordination, and theme execution.

"Of course, it does, dear. And don't even think about stealing any of my ideas," Lorraine playfully warned, emerging from her bedroom at the back of the unit.

"You know I was raised better than that, Mom. When I put my decorations us, they're going to blow you away. And if there happens to be any similarity, it's just because we share the same impeccable taste," Melissa responded with a smile.

"Mmmhmm, sounds to me like you're already crafting excuses to borrow my style," Lorraine said teasingly before turning more serious. "Maybe if you spent less time here after work and more at your place, you'd have your decorations up by now."

Lorraine, a fierce holiday decorator, firmly believed in having Christmas decorations up before the end of the Thanksgiving weekend. While this was a common American tradition, it had only become Lorraine's practice after her divorce from Melissa's father. Before the divorce, he had insisted on delaying any Christmas decorations until the week before the holiday, disliking the commercialization of the season. Changing this tradition was Lorraine's first act of independence, allowing her to celebrate as she wished for the first time in her life.

"Mom, some mothers would love to have a daughter who visits as much as I do," Melissa argued.

"Not when their daughter uses those visits to avoid her own life," Lorraine countered with a smirk. "Your prolonged visits border on harassment, especially when you should be hanging out with your best friend who is also single."

Melissa suppressed a sigh. Her mother knew that she did not like being referred to as single. She was a widow and that was different from being single. She was still mourning her husband. Rather than reminding her mother of that, Melissa shifted the topic to her reason for visiting.

"I know, Mom. I just came to tell you about a new resident moving in down the hall. Maybe you'd like to meet him and show him around once his son leaves."

"And why should I do that? Isn't giving a tour part of your job?" Lorraine asked sharply. She could see where this conversation was heading and swiftly put a stop to it. "I'll encounter him soon enough around here. You should focus that matchmaking energy on your own love life instead of trying to pair me up with someone."

At sixty-seven, Lorraine was as outspoken as ever. Age had only made her more candid, expressing her thoughts freely at any given moment. Aware that Melissa had given up on love after Maurice died, Lorraine often redirected her daughter's attempts at matchmaking back onto Melissa herself.

Melissa didn't think her mother needed help in the romance department. Lorraine was attractive, financially stable, humorous, and shared a passion for sports on par with most men. She had always been independent, not one to cling to her partner, as she had her own life to manage. If only Melissa's father, Edward, hadn't mistaken Lorraine's kindness for weakness and strayed, they might still have been happily married. But Lorraine was someone who didn't forgive what she considered to be unforgivable. She firmly believed in not giving anyone a second chance to break her heart, which was why she disapproved of Melissa considering a reconciliation with Maurice.

"But, Mom, it's not like Maurice cheated on me," Melissa defended, referring to Maurice's marriage to his first wife.

"Maybe not," Lorraine countered, "but he knew you were waiting for him. He knew he could leave her, and you would take him back instantly. A man should never be so sure of your love. It gives them too much power – power they can't handle and don't deserve."

Lorraine had expressed these sentiments when Melissa first told her about her plans to marry Maurice on Christmas. Despite her mother's warnings, Melissa's love for Maurice had driven her to take that leap of faith. Yet, in the end, she was hurt, although not due to any fault of Maurice's.

Focusing on her love life was the last thing Melissa wanted. It was far easier to concentrate on the happiness of others, the residents of Rose Garden, including her mother whether Lorraine liked it or not.

Feeling uneasy at the discussion of her romantic past, Melissa shifted in her suede blazer and chose not to argue further. "You're right. You will meet Mr. Walker soon enough. I'm going to check on them one more time before I head home. I bet you'll be glad to see me leave."

"I'll be happier to see you going on a date," Lorraine quipped with a smile that Melissa turned her back on.

"Have a good evening, Mom."

The two Phillips were working in perfect succinctness when Melissa peeked her head in the door. The senior of the two was handling the lightweight stuff, putting towels and bedding in the linen closet, while the younger one was opening the boxes of kitchen items and putting them in their proper places. Their conversation was light and playful like she and her mothers were when the subject wasn't either of their love lives. She could feel the closeness between them. Not wanting to stop the efficient flow of the two Phillips, Melissa called out a quick goodbye and then headed to her office for her things.

Scene 4

IT WAS JUST AFTER SEVEN o'clock when Melissa keyed in the four-digit code on the keypad to unlock her home's entry door. As expected, her honey-colored Cocker Spaniel, Peanut, was eagerly panting as Melissa closed the door behind her. Peanut knew the smaller bag in Melissa's left hand contained his Friday night snack.

Melissa had been visiting the new Thai restaurant around the corner from her Southfield home every Friday. After a week of avoiding carbs, her favorite Thai entrée—Pineapple Fried Rice, was a welcomed treat. On her first visit to the restaurant, Peanut was sitting in her lap when the manager, Jocelyn, and a proclaimed lover of Cocker Spaniels, brought her food out. Now Jocelyn included a treat for Peanut whenever Melissa called in an order.

If Melissa hadn't been cautious of the excited twenty-pound furbaby circling her feet, she might have tripped over her on her way to the kitchen.

"Okay, baby girl! I know you want your treat, but there's no need to act like you haven't eaten all day."

Melissa spoke to the dog as though she were a person who could return the dialogue. Melissa made sure that Peanut did not go hungry or get too lonely during the day while she was at work. When she'd inherited the dog from one of her neighbors who passed away two years ago, Melissa made a conscious decision to be one of *those* pet owners—the ones who celebrate their pet's birthday, buy them silly but adorable costumes for Halloween and other holidays, and hire a dog walker. Kiada, a 20-year-old Black Asian college student who started a dog-walking business as a side-hustle to help with tuition costs, came over every day to walk Peanut for thirty minutes while Melissa was at work.

Melissa placed her bags on the grey and white granite kitchen countertop. She then stooped down to affectionately rub the top of Peanut's furry head, before tenderly scooping the dog into her arms.

"Aww, I know you missed mommy," she cooed softly to Peanut. "I missed you too, baby." And she genuinely meant it. Since the loss of Maurice, Peanut was the only new living being to whom Melissa had opened her heart. Loving her furry companion was the only risk she felt willing to take with her heart these days.

Sometimes Melissa worried about something happening to Peanut. She had known other pet parents who had suffered the loss of their beloved pets due to old age or, in some tragic cases, accidents like being hit by a car or ingesting something poisonous. She had observed their deep sorrow yet couldn't quite equate it with the pain of losing a spouse, a parent, or a child. Over time, these pet owners often, after several months or perhaps a year or two, brought a new pet into their homes.

While they cherished the memories of their departed pets, they seemed to move on to lead happy, new lives.

However, for Melissa, no one could ever take Maurice's place. Not even someone as strikingly attractive and well put together as Mr. Paul Walker Jr., or P.J., as he had indicated. Melissa might have closed her heart to love, but her eyesight was perfectly intact. And P.J., she mused, was undoubtedly fine, with a capital 'F.' Dressed in his grey sweat suit, his muscular build was not just evident, but also a pleasing sight. Fortunately for her, he bore a striking resemblance, albeit a younger version, to his father. And that was precisely why Melissa decided to channel her efforts into fostering a connection, whether it be love or just friendly companionship, between the senior Paul Walker and her mother.

When Peanut rested her head on top of Melissa's shoulder, she knew it was safe to put her down and give her the treat she was waiting for. Now Melissa could relax on the couch with her Friday night meal and a glass of her favorite sweet red wine and try to avoid looking at the space in her living room where her Christmas tree and decorations were supposed to be.

She hated lying to her mother about decorating for the holidays, particularly the Christmas holiday. This was *their* thing. Had been since she was a little girl, followed by friendly competition when Melissa had gotten her own place. But reuniting with Maurice and marrying him on Christmas day, followed by the devastation of his death, had dulled her festiveness. Weirdly, she could enjoy decorating in her workplace with her employees, which is why she was so annoyed that they did it without her.

But at home, alone, she couldn't even stand the sight of the decorations. It made sense the first year after Maurice died when she was still living in the house that they shared. But by year two, she had sold that home and bought another to rid herself of the memories of him. Obviously, that hadn't worked. Maybe Alanna, her best friend, was right when she said, "I think you defeated the purpose of starting over in a new home with all these pictures you plastered of the two of you in every corner of the house."

Melissa forgave Alanna's insensitive statement. Some of the ladies in the online widow support group that she frequented every other Friday talked all the time about the crazy and insensitive things well-meaning friends and family often said to grieving widows. So, Melissa imagined them rooting her on when responding to Alanna's statement.

"It's never been my intention to forget about Maurice. He'll always hold a special place in my heart." She held on to these words with as much conviction today as she did four years ago, when she first uttered them to Alanna. Sitting in the very same living room now, memories flooded back. As was her routine at the onset of the holiday season, Melissa found solace in stretching out on the microfiber suede red couch. Here, she would sleep the weekend away, seeking solace in her dreams until she could return to her work, the only place where she found genuine happiness.

Scene 5

P.J., TRUDGED THROUGH the front door of his house after a long day of unpacking and setting up his father's new residence. He had not anticipated the overwhelming sense of guilt that washed over him as he left Phillip Sr. in what was to be his new home—a home devoid of any memories of his mother. This realization pained him deeply. As he fought back a solitary tear, he felt like a hypocrite. He remembered comforting Felicia about her guilt concerning their father's move to a senior home.

The Rose Garden residence, despite its homey aura, could not possibly match the warmth and familiarity of the home he grew up visiting. First with both parents and later just his father. He resolved to visit as often as his hectic schedule allowed, both to familiarize himself with the new setting and, if he was completely honest with himself, to admire Mrs. Fields, the owner. P.J. wasn't looking for a relationship but that didn't stop him from appreciating a beautiful woman.

In his line of work, he encountered many attractive women, yet none captivated him quite like Mrs. Fields. Her brown skin, reminiscent of golden sand, and her round eyes, subtly lined with dark brown eyeliner and a hint of shimmery dust on her eyelids, left a lasting impression. The light makeup she wore enhanced her undeniable natural beauty, embodying the concept that 'less is more'. He admired the confidence she exuded with this understated approach to beauty.

But Mrs. Fields' confidence was evident beyond her pretty face. The fact that she'd had the courage to enter the senior care industry as an African American woman was courageous and admirable. He didn't have to Google it to know there were fewer Black women owned and managed senior care facilities. It was impressive that she had the will and finances to open her establishment. He was proud of her without even knowing her. And no woman he'd come across in recent years had that effect on him. Her husband was lucky to have her.

"Alright, man, it's time to get her out of your head," P.J. spoke aloud to himself. Having dutifully fulfilled his obligations as a son, his focus now shifted to the administrative tasks required for his business. This transition in thought inadvertently brought his mother's words to the forefront of his mind.

"Son, you're constantly working. What's the point of possessing the whole world if there's no one to share it with? Don't let life just pass you by," she would often say. Like his father, she harbored a deep desire to see him settled down with a family. Her encouragement, however, was always tinged with a biblical perspective.

P.J. valued his parents' concern for his personal life. However, he was aware that neither of them had ever navigated the complexities of owning a business. They believed that since his sister managed to run a successful salon while maintaining a family life, P.J. should be able to do the same. But he recognized that there was a stark difference between his sister Felicia's business and his own.

Felicia's salon operated on fixed hours and focused primarily on hair services. In contrast, his work as a contractor demanded flexibility to adapt to varying environmental conditions. For instance, he often worked on Saturdays to preempt the harsh, unpredictable weather typical in Michigan during fall and winter.

Then there were times when he had to fulfill tight deadlines he had promised to his clients, leading to workdays stretching ten to twelve hours. During such periods, he appreciated the presence of his students. He aimed to demonstrate to them that they didn't have to conform to the negative stereotypes often associated with contractors, such as being inconsiderate of clients' time.

P.J. was acutely aware of the numerous factors outside a contractor's control—weather conditions, fluctuating material costs, labor availability, and so forth. This understanding guided his approach to job forecasting. When quoting a project, he meticulously reviewed his staff availability, weather forecasts, material suppliers, and other relevant factors, incorporating a buffer for unforeseen issues instead of simply proposing an optimistic completion date to please the client. This thoroughness was reflected in his customer reviews, highlighting the appreciation clients had for his company's reliability. Many repeat customers were even willing to wait for his schedule to clear for non-urgent jobs. This level of customer trust and loyalty was why he dedicated weekends to revisiting ongoing projects, reevaluating his availability, and personally reaching out to clients on his waiting list, a task typically handled by his answering service.

"There's work to be done, Mom," he said aloud to his mother's memory. *The day I come across a woman who understands that a successful business doesn't exist without sacrifices, I will then consider marriage.* He clicked the "Messages" folder on his iPad and started reading.

If Melissa weren't a consummate professional, she would have done the electric slide through the doors of Rose Garden when she arrived at work the following Monday morning. She was *that* happy to return to her happy place of work. The blistering cold and quarter-size snow flurries that were dropping from the sky and sticking to the ground did not alter her mood.

"Good morning, Mr. Binion," she smiled, handing him a cup of black coffee.

"Morning, Ms. Fields," he said, nodding his thanks for the coffee she handed him as she dashed by him for the elevator. In her office, she hung her coat on the rack in the corner, sat in her chair, and then powered on her computer. Once it was on, she clicked on the icon to check her email and calendar.

Holiday Rehearsal

Ouch. It was a reminder she did not want. Engrossed in the bustling activity of the new resident move-in, it had completely escaped her notice until this very moment that only one of the three contractors she had scheduled for last Friday had shown up. And although she expected as much, there was one company she was most disappointed in.

One Source Contracting.

The glowing testimonials featured on their website had raised her expectations tremendously. Past customers had enthusiastically praised their timeliness, professionalism, creativity, and the superior quality of work delivered by the owner and his crew. If no other company had shown up that day, this wasn't the company she expected to be.

After settling in at her desk, Melissa performed a Google search of each of the companies scheduled that day. She clicked the "review" section of each and typed out her disappointment in their no-shows. But, for One Source, she was notably more severe in her critique. Clearly, there had been a drastic decline in their standards, and she felt compelled to share her experience, determined to alert other unsuspecting prospective customers to this disappointing change.

Don't be fooled by the glowing reviews you see here. Not professional at all. I had an appointment for a consultation this past Friday, and the proprietor never showed up.
He didn't even bother calling to say he couldn't make it.

A small wave of relief fell on her after she pressed enter on the review she just typed, but she was still irritated. She didn't know what irritated her most: the lack of professionalism of these contractors or the likelihood that she had made a promise to her staff and residents that she might not be able to keep.

Unprofessionalism made her skin crawl, but her heart ached at the possibility of letting down her residents and staff. Everybody had been so excited with those first few rehearsals that they had had. Mr. Washington, from 2B, was preparing a comedy skit. Delores and her husband Brian were ball room dancing. Donna and Susan, both staff members, were performing a lip-sync battle of pop Christmas music while her mom and two other residents were singing a string of Motown Christmas hits. Melissa was livid that she had let everybody, including herself, get excited, and now it may not have been happening.

That was exactly the issue she was discussing with her mother in the resident dining hall when Paul Walker, the new resident, spontaneously decided to join their table.

"Do you lovely ladies mind if I join you?" he inquired, already comfortably seated before they could respond.

"Please, join us," Lorraine encouraged, exchanging a meaningful glance across the table with Melissa. "Perhaps you could even help me convince my daughter here that installing a stage for our senior citizens to enjoy some much-needed fun isn't necessary. She tends to be overly particular about these things."

"Well, I wouldn't want to create any tension between mother and daughter by taking sides," Paul interjected with a smile, "but I might just have a practical solution. My son is a general contractor, and I'm confident he could construct a small, yet functional stage quite efficiently."

Melissa's eyes sparkled with interest. "He is?" Her mind drifted back to their brief interaction during the move-in. She struggled to recall any specifics he might have shared about himself, but his handsome features were not easily forgotten. "I had no idea."

"Indeed, he is," Paul confirmed. "His schedule has been quite full recently, but I'm sure he could make time for this. He'll be here soon to drop off some of my belongings that were left in his truck. We can discuss it with him then."

"That sounds wonderful," Melissa responded eagerly. "I really hope he can help us out. I want this so much for everyone here," she said, gesturing towards the other residents in the dining hall.

"And in the meantime, we can continue practicing in the open space of the recreation room, stage or no stage," Lorraine suggested, just as Melissa's walkie-talkie buzzed at her hip. "Yes?" she answered, ready to tend to the call.

"Nadine, in 3D, would like to see you if you're available." Darlene's voice came clear through the communication gadget.

"Sure. I'll be right there," Melissa responded. "Mom, I'll check on you a little later. Enjoy your breakfast. You too, Mr. Walker. And, please, let me know when your son comes through."

"Will do," Mr. Walker said with a smile.

It turns out that Nadine didn't want anything. She just wanted to show off her Christmas decorations in her unit. It seemed like some of her residents just liked to get some face-to-face time with her, especially since she gave so much attention to her mother. She briefly toyed with the idea of cutting back on visits to her mother, just in case it was a jealousy thing, but that thought didn't last long. Seeing her mother often was the very reason she insisted her mother become a resident in her place of business. So, if she had to accommodate the few residents, like Nadine, who wanted some special attention of their own, she was willing to do that.

On her way back to her office, an alluring scent of cologne filled her nostrils just as she nearly collided with the junior Mr. Walker. Underneath his gray overcoat, he wore faded jeans and heavy-looking work boots. The infamous English D, representing Detroit, was emblazoned on the skullcap covering his head.

"Oh, excuse me!" she gushed apologetically. "Oh. Mr. Walker. I was hoping to see you today."

His brown eyes smiled. "That's a nice change from our first encounter when you preferred my sister over me."

Melissa blushed with embarrassment, though she was sure he was not *that* offended. "Hopefully, it helps that you were a pleasant surprise." She said, in a flirty voice that she hadn't heard out of her mouth in ages.

OMG. What has gotten into me? She thought. Not only was this her new resident's parent, but she simply should not be playing like that with this very handsome guy when she was not in the market for dating.

"Umm... what I meant is that I was talking to your father today, and he indicated that you might be able to help me with something that I need."

"Okay. Speaking of my father, I'm trying to find him. Maybe you can help me out with that while we talk about how I can help you," he suggested.

"Sounds like a win-win," she replied, her voice taking on a forced professional tone. "I can walk you to where he was last, which was the dining hall, and if he's not there, I'll take you to his unit. On the way, I can show you what I need."

"Sure," he said, and they began walking together.

As they walked down the hall toward the dining hall, their arms grazed each other. He was a few inches taller than her five four height. *Same as Maurice,* she thought reluctantly but surprised. Whenever she was in the presence of black men, she tended to notice what was similar or dissimilar to her late husband. She couldn't say whether that was good or bad, especially three years into her widow's journey, but it was what it was for her. She was glad to return her thoughts to the present when they came to the recreation room.

"You see, I had this idea to construct a stage in this space. Given the size of the room, it still leaves plenty of space for walking, dancing, and the tables that the residents use for all sorts of activities. The staff and residents have already been practicing for the Christmas extravaganza I promised them, and that's why time is of the essence. But your father insisted that, since it's not a huge job, you might be able to get this done for me."

P.J. didn't respond immediately. Instead, he walked around the space, looking at it speculatively. He inhaled deeply before saying, "I won't say it's such a small job. But in all good conscience, I can't turn down the woman who is essentially responsible for my father's well-being. Plus, it's the holiday season," he added, revealing a friendly smile.

"While I'm glad that my role in your father's life provides me some preferential treatment, I don't want you to take on more than you can handle. I know how busy things have gotten for general contractors." She opted not to delve into her recent contractor experiences.

"Don't worry about that. I pride myself on keeping my schedule manageable, so I don't get bogged down and can't supply superb service on the front and back end. Before I commit, I'll check my calendar and get back to you by tomorrow's close of business. How's that sound?"

"I love it. Thank you!"

"Great. In the meantime, keep your staff and residents rehearsing. And since my dad likes to offer my services, let me tell you that he does a mean impression of Berry White."

"Is that so?" She asked speculatively.

He winked at her, and she nodded her head in the direction of his father.

Luckily, the senior Paul was in his unit when she knocked on the door. And surprisingly, so was her mother. She wanted her mother to befriend the new resident but didn't expect it to be so soon *and* without her interference.

"And what's going on in here?" Melissa asked, exchanging a quizzical look with junior Paul.

"Isn't that obvious with all the Christmas decorations?" Her mother quipped. "Paul was feeling a little left out of the holiday spirit, so I offered him some of my extra Christmas decor as well as some of my decorating expertise."

"That's awfully nice of you, mom." Melissa directed her next words to Mr. Walker. "Paul, you should consider yourself lucky. My mom does not usually share her decorating expertise. It's part of her competitive nature."

"I didn't know it was a contest."

"Yep. I decided that just now. It can be a part of the Christmas extravaganza. I'm thinking we can record videos of everyone's interior decorations and create a slide presentation. Maybe have some guest judges."

"Well, since you want to be funny, I expect footage of your decorations at home for this random contest," Lorraine said in a challenging tone that insinuated that she knew that Melissa hadn't put up one iota of decorations in her house and the reason behind it.

Realizing she may have just put her foot in her mouth, she decided to sidestep the topic of decorations.

"Well, as promised, Mr. Walker, I have assisted you in locating your father. And I hope it works out for you to be able to assist me with the stage. Do you happen to have a card I can take back to my office?"

"Sure." He pulled out a brown leather wallet from his back pocket and handed her a card he fished out of it.

"Thank you. Mom, Mr. Walker," She turned back to her mother, who was arranging garland along the wall. "I'll leave you to your decorating. Call you later."

Scene 6

WHILE HIS FATHER AND Ms. Lorraine were engrossed in decorating the unit, P.J. busied himself with anything else he could find. He was glad his father was settling in so soon and enjoying his new environment, but it was slightly uncomfortable witnessing this enjoyment in the company of a woman other than his mother.

Flashes of him and his sister helping their mother decorate the Christmas tree when they were little passed through his mind. It was a whole production. They wore Santa hats with their names written in glitter across the front and blasted the Jackson 5 Christmas album as they danced around the tree. P.J.'s favorite time was when his mother would chase his father around the house whenever *I Saw Mommy Kissing Santa Claus*, planting kisses all over his face when she caught him. And she always caught him. He wanted to be caught. It was part of the show. The memory was full blown when his father returned from walking Ms. Lorraine back to her unit.

"The place looks great. Festive. As if mom had her hand on it herself." P.J. said, blinking back tears.

"I know. She was not far from my thoughts as Lorraine and I were decorating. But I know she was smiling down on me, enjoying myself a little. Even in the company of another woman."

"Pops," P.J. cocked his head to the side. "You just moved in here a few days ago. I know you're not pushing up on this woman already?"

"Hey, I know what to do when I come across an attractive woman. I'm not sure what your problem is, son." Mr. Walker quipped.

"Oh. Is that what you call yourself doing recommending me for work with Mrs. Fields so I would spend more time with her? If you hadn't noticed the "Mrs" as part of her title. As attractive as the woman is, she's married."

"Actually, she isn't." Paul Sr said, puffing his chest out proudly. "According to her mother, she's widowed. But I'm glad you're not too caught up in your business to notice that she's attractive."

"Okay. A widow who still wears a ring." P.J. said skeptically.

"Mmmhmm. Holding out on me, huh? I see in the short time you've been acquainted with Mrs. Fields, you noticed that she was wearing a ring. Interesting."

"I am a man before anything. It's only natural to check out an attractive woman. But I'm sure that a widow, still wearing her wedding ring, is not in the market for dating. So, your motive for recommending me for this job is moot."

"I disagree. It might not help your love life, but it can move mine in the right direction with her mother."

"Okay. I'm done with this conversation. I need to get to work. And on top of that, now I need to try to squeeze in another job, thanks to you."

"Complain about it now, but you might be thanking me later." Paul Sr said as P.J. closed the door behind him.

Scene 7

"SO, I SEE YOU OPENED your big mouth to my mother," Melissa said to her best friend, Alanna. They had met for dinner at a Thai restaurant after work.

"What are you talking about?" Alanna said, shifting her eyes, feigning innocence.

"Whatever!"

"Okay, okay. But you know how your mom can be. She always calls me to check on you when she believes you're not being forthcoming. I tried to cover for you, but she busted me by asking me to send her just one picture that I had taken."

That would do it. Alanna was the kind of person who took pictures of everything—things she liked and things she didn't. She had already taken multiple pictures of the two of them sitting together at their table and of their food.

"Fine. I get it. I just wish you had told me, or I wouldn't have opened my own big mouth about a holiday decorating contest. Now, not only am I stuck with this contest, but I'm also stuck with this unprofessional contractor."

"Why are you stuck with him?

"First, because he's available. He left me a message before I left work that he would be able to fit my job in next Tuesday and be finished by Friday, which is perfect timing. Second, because he's my new resident's son, we're going to be seeing each other after the fact. And third, he's my new resident's son. A resident that my mother seems to like. I didn't even have to pull out my match-making skills. They naturally gravitated to each other. So, I can't fire the man before he starts because I know how he operates."

When Melissa returned to her office, she took some calls and reviewed recent emails from the state. Then she pulled out the business card P.J. had given her.

One Source Contracting.

A surge went through her body at the recognition of the name. That company with glowing reviews was amongst those contractors that stood her up. She couldn't believe the nerve of Mr. Paul Walker Jr. coming up in here trying to pose himself off as a consummate professional with his, *'I pride myself on keeping a manageable schedule. Blah Blah. Blah.'* So much for his manageable schedule if he couldn't keep a simple consultation appointment. What could she expect from his actual work? How could she be sure he wouldn't start building the stage and then stop for whatever reason and leave her with a bigger mess?

"I know how much of a stickler you are about professionalism, but maybe you should consider that it was an oversight because his mind may have been on this transition with his father. You know that's possible." Alanna said in P.J.'s defense.

Of course, she thought about that *after* she realized that P.J. was the proprietor of One Source Contracting. But that fact did not mean anything at the realization of being blown off.

"I understand, however, that is why business owners need to have assistants. Hence, I've started my search before my current one goes on maternity leave. I mean, a sole proprietor cannot do everything, at least not do everything well. And who suffers when they try to do it all? Their customers, or, in my case, potential customers."

"Well, you're a customer now," Alanna said pointedly. "And I think you should cut the brother, an attractive brother, I might add, a little slack. He could be the one to brighten your holiday season in more ways than one."

"Ohmigod!" Melissa threw her head back. "I see you and my mother had quite the conversation. Only she could have told you that the man is handsome, which has nothing to do with his work ethic, *I* might add."

"Your mom and I just care about you. We are both looking forward to the day you open your heart to love again. You deserve that." The last words Alanna said were soft and genuine. But neither of them understood what it was like to lose a spouse. Her mother was happily divorced, and Alanna had never been married. Melissa didn't feel like explaining her disinterest in love during the holiday season or any other time.

Scene 8

P.J. HAD TO DO SOME creative finagling of his workmen's schedules to free up two of them to help him with the last-minute scheduled job at Rose Garden.

"So, who is she?" Brian asked when he climbed into the passenger side of the work truck.

"What are you talking about, B? P.J. asked seriously.

"I'm just saying. Since we started working after Covid, you've been stringent about the job schedule, and I haven't known you to make an exception with this kind of short notice," Brian said, side-eyeing P.J. "I can't imagine it being anything but a fine woman who made you bend the rules."

P.J. laughed mostly under his breath. Brian was a newbie. He couldn't have been further off with his presumption about why P.J. made an exception for Mrs. Fields. Yes, she was beautiful. But that was the last thing on his mind when he looked for an opening in his schedule. He would have done the same if she looked like the Grinch. The last time he veered from making a business decision with the wrong head, he almost lost his business. He vowed to never do that again.

"Naw, buddy. Her looks had nothing to do with the exception. Things just work in her favor."

Mmmhmm," Brian scolded. "That means she's fine."

P.J. scoffed before returning his focus to the road ahead of him. They arrived at Rose Garden twenty minutes later. Mrs. Fields met them at the door. Unlike the first two times he'd seen her, the brightness was missing from her eyes, and her stature was as cold as the twenty-five degrees it was outside.

"Good morning," he said.

"Good morning, Mr. Walker," she replied icily. "I'll walk you over to the rec room. I'm sure you don't remember where it is." She added, taking short, quick steps, expecting them to follow, which they did.

"This is my workman, Brian, who's going to be working with me today," P.J. explained, not because it wasn't obvious, but to fill the silence as they walked along.

"Okay, here we are," she said crisply when they arrived at the rec room. "I sent notices to the residents that the rec room is off limits for the three days that you stated it would take to finish the job. Please don't make a liar out of me to my staff and residents. I'd really appreciate it." She added before turning swiftly and walking away.

Wow. What the hell was that about? P.J. thought to himself.

Melissa slumped in her chair when she was in her office. She knew she had not been kind to the junior Mr. Walker. A week had passed since she realized he was another contractor who had disappointed her. But she could not be sure if she was annoyed by that fact, or if it was the Facebook memory she was confronted with over the weekend. As soon as she opened the app on her phone, a picture of her and Maurice picking out their first Christmas tree together covered her screen. Alanna had taken the picture. The memory sent shockwaves through her body and brought instant tears to her eyes. She crawled back under her covers and did not resurface until this morning.

Returning to work did not lift her spirits as it usually did. Her mood was flat as a pancake. She did not even buy Mr. Binion a coffee like she usually did, which saddened her because she enjoyed brightening people's days. That's why she went into this line of work: bringing joy to others made her feel better on her worst days. Usually.

Melissa spent most of the day hibernating in her office, emerging only if a pressing matter demanded her attention. She knew she should have gone to check on the men working, but she was embarrassed about her behavior that morning. Instead, she sent her very pregnant assistant, Rebecca, to do the deed. And then she felt bad about that too. The day was going from bad to worse.

A knock on the door snapped her to attention.

"Yes," she called out.

"There's a delivery for you," Rebecca said through the door.

A delivery. Residents in the building received things all the time, but those things were delivered directly to their units.

"Come on in."

When the door opened, Rebecca was not alone. Melissa's mother, Mr. Binion, and Deneen were shuffling into her office in a half circle. Everyone wore goofy smiles.

"What is going on?" Melissa demanded to know.

"This!" Her mother squealed the loudest as their circle opened to reveal a large bouquet mixed with pink and yellow carnations, strawberries and pineapple chunks.

"Oh wow. These are for me?" She asked skeptically.

"Girl, do you think we'd be in here like this if they weren't?" Her mother said sassily.

"I guess not. But why all the fanfare? It's not like no one has ever sent me a token of their appreciation."

"Yeah, but this token is from a gentleman caller. In fact, the handsome guy downstairs, swinging the hammer for the stage you asked for."

"What?" Melissa stood to receive the bouquet. It was beautiful. There was no denying that. But if it was indeed from the junior Mr. Walker or his workman and it was just another display of this man's lack of professionalism.

"Thank you for the delivery. I'll make sure to thank Mr. Walker on my way out," Melissa said flatly.

"On your way out?" Her mother said. "That's not for another hour. You should go and thank him now while he's still here. For all you know, he could be gone before you decide to leave here today.

Maybe moving her here wasn't such a good idea, Melissa thought as she obediently stood up behind her desk.

"Fine, but I'm only going now so I don't appear rude. *Not* because you told me to."

"Whatever you must tell yourself. Just don't run away from the first man to show you some attention."

Melissa did not confirm whether her mother's statement was accurate or not. Instead, she walked out of her office, forcing a toothy "hello" to residents that she passed along the way to the rec center. Her mother's words swirled in her head.

"Don't run away from the first man to show you some kindness."

Melissa was searching her memory bank for the last time a man hit on her when she nearly collided with the junior Mr. Walker *again*.

"We must stop meeting like this," he said, placing her hands on both of her shoulders to steady her.

"I agree," she replied, brushing her hands nervously down her legs. "Uhh, I was coming down to thank you for the edible arrangements you sent to my office."

"Oh, you're wel..."

"But" she said interrupting him. "It was quite unprofessional. This is my business, and I would have appreciated a romantic gesture of flowers being sent to my home."

"Romantic gesture?" He said, surprised. "I think you have misunderstood my intentions. Did you read the card?"

"Card?" She hadn't seen a card. "No, I didn't."

"Well, that would have been helpful. Here's what the card said." He pulled out his phone, and after a couple of clicks, he held up the screen to the online order he sent to the company.

Greetings, Mrs. Field,

Please accept this token of thanks for allowing One Source Contracting

to service your needs this holiday season.

Owner/Proprietor,

Paul Walker Jr.

"Oh," she said softly. "Nothing unprofessional about that," she admitted.

"Nope. Not at all." P.J. said through tightened lips. "We've only got another couple of hours left before we're finished for the day."

A wave of guilt washed over her as he turned to get back to work. "Umm, Mr. Walker," she called to him. "I apologize for jumping to conclusions, but I had a little help. My staff and my mother kind of made a big deal about the delivery because it was from you. They made it into something else, and the note attached was suspiciously not there when they gave it to me."

"So, without a note, you assumed the worst?" He asked speculatively.

"Well..." she began before he interjected.

"The worst by your standards. Because it would have made me a terrible and unprofessional person to have wanted to brighten your day, which must not be going well judging from your rough exterior this morning. You have a good evening, Mrs. Field," he said, turning his back to her and going back to work.

Act 2

Scene 1

Over the next two days, P.J. and Brian arrived each day at precisely 9 am and wrapped up at 4 pm. They meticulously cleaned up behind themselves. Some of her residents commented how much they appreciated that the rec room didn't look like an eyesore just while it was being worked on.

Melissa wouldn't know herself because she avoided the rec room like the plaque after Mr. Walker properly checked her for her negative assumption. Plus, she really couldn't be sure if he was just being a nice guy or *if* some romantic interest lurked behind the gesture. His explanation had been inconclusive. He could have wanted to brighten her day professionally or personally. She made it clear that she wasn't comfortable with that latter.

P.J. was proud of the stage he and Brian constructed for the residents of Rose Garden. Ms. Fields had been a visionary for wanting it built. Sure, she wanted it for the residents to have their Christmas program, but P.J. saw it being more than that.

He imagined local performers being able to come in for the entertainment of the residents. Comedians, musicians, singers. He knew a handful of people in those circles who would love to donate their time for the entertainment of the seniors. He would have to share his thoughts with his father in hopes of him sharing it with Ms. Lorraine and then her sharing it with her daughter. It was a lot of hoops to relay a simple suggestion, but the way Ms. Fields avoided him after checking him about the arrangement he sent to her office, he got the clear message that she did not want to be bothered, at least not with him.

"Another job completed on the books," he said to Brian as they gathered up scrap materials to throw in the dumpster.

"Yeah, you can put me on all the easy jobs like this. Indoors, too? Sign me up." Brian was saying.

"I can't guarantee the next job will be as easy, but there's definitely more jobs coming down the pipes."

Scene 2

"WELL, BABY GIRL, I see you went and did exactly the opposite of what I told you to do," Lorraine was saying from the passenger seat of Melissa's car. "I remember you being a much more obedient child when you were younger."

"You mean when I was actually a child?" Melissa dared to say.

"Girrlll, I know you think I won't pop you because you're driving," Lorraine retorted.

Melissa smiled a short smile. "Ok, but for real, Mom, there are only so many things you can still tell me what to do and expect me to actually do it. My personal life is not one of them. Furthermore, maybe if you all hadn't instigated removing his note from the arrangement, I would have known that his intentions weren't as unprofessional as I thought."

Lorraine sighed heavily. "His intentions were kind either way you look at it, and if you had just said "thank you" as I told you to, who knows where it would have gone from there? He could have been taking you to a nice dinner instead of you spending the day with me thrift shopping."

"But I love thrift shopping with you. Plus, it's even more exciting today because we're hunting for evening gowns for your upcoming performance!"

After P.J. finished with the stage, Melissa summoned the residents down that evening for a grand reveal of sorts. Everybody was so excited and unanimously voted to dress up for their performances. Melissa volunteered her and her mom to hit up all the thrift stores in the area and a few that she didn't mind driving the distance for to gather as many wardrobes the following weekend. That's what the two of them were doing today.

"Yes, this is fun, but you need more of what a man like P.J. could bring into your life."

"Mom! Really? What do you really know about him besides the fact that he is attractive?"

"Similar to yourself, he is a successful business owner. He's single, more focused on his business instead of womanizing like he could be. He's a homeowner of a beautiful home, which, according to his father, is ready for the right woman to come to nurture it and fill it with a couple of children. And you know a man who builds things is likely good with his hands in other areas."

"Okay, Mom," Melissa's cheeks burned with embarrassment. "Conversation over!"

Four hours later and their thrifting mission was deemed a success. They returned to Rose Garden with enough variations of long and short rhinestones and silk dresses, suede and leather suit jackets for the men, dazzling jewelry options, and accessories for everyone who was participating in the Christmas extravaganza. All for under two dollars! The simple addition of the stage was leading the Christmas program that Melissa expected to be simple holiday fun for the residents to be a highly anticipated event for residents, staff, and their families.

Scene 3

FRIDAY, DECEMBER 18th, was the night of the performance. So many people had RSVP'd for the event as of yesterday that Melissa hired a company to bring extra chairs to accommodate. They arrived at noon and had everything set up within thirty minutes. Alanna, who also moonlighted as a caterer, arrived on time at three p.m. with subs, individual bags of chips, a veggie tray, and pop. She was dressed and ready for showtime at five p.m.

Melissa managed to finagle herself into the show as the co-emcee for the night along with Alanna. She had bought a gold shimmery mini dress that she had been dying to wear for a special occasion.

By five p.m. the rec room was filled with more people than it had ever hosted before. Melissa couldn't stop smiling. She welcomed everyone to the show and then turned it over to Alanna so she could mingle with the people who had entrusted her with the care of their family members.

As she worked the room, shaking hands and hugging long-time residents and family members, expressing her thanks for their attendance, she was thoroughly entertained by each performer. The renditions of The Temptations, The Supremes, and The Four Tops were impeccable. She stood at the back of the room for her mom's performance, giving it her undivided attention. Over the four minutes of the performance, their roles seemed to reverse, and Melissa was like the proud mother of her child. And, just like a mother, she didn't miss the googly eyes her mother was making at the senior Mr. Walker, who was watching the performance from the front row.

Melissa also noticed that the junior Mr. Walker was seated next to his father and a slightly younger woman who shared a family resemblance. *Felicia*. The sister, Melissa, presumed. She'd forgotten how much she was looking forward to meeting Felicia the day she ended up meeting her brother. It was her first time seeing him since the edible arrangement incident. When the stage had been completed, she'd made an excuse to leave the building so that Deneen would be authorized on her behalf to approve and sign off on the job as complete. She instructed Deneen to take pictures, but Melissa had no doubts that it would be exactly what she wanted. Plus, every evening after Mr. Walker and his partner had left for the day, she would take a walk down to the rec room and inspect the work. Not to mention the residents who went on and on about how it was looking whenever they encountered her.

She let her eyes rest on him too long as he shifted uncomfortably in his chair and then looked in her direction. Their eyes locked in for a moment before she snapped her head back toward the stage to focus on the next performer.

The last performer ended at six forty-five, and it was time for a little surprise that she planned for her residents and staff. She planned this surprise before the inception of the stage, *before* the incident with the junior Mr. Walker. She considered canceling it, especially when she knew he would likely be there for the show considering his father was one of the performers. But she certainly didn't expect him to be in the front row!

Melissa inhaled slowly and exhaled even slower as she stepped onto that stage.

"Good evening, everyone," she said gleefully, projecting her voice to reach the back of the room. "Hasn't this been a fantastic night?" she asked, eliciting a mighty applause.

"Let's give all our performers a round of applause. Without their enthusiastic commitment to participate and all their practices over the last couple of weeks, this night would not have been possible. So, I say thank you, thank you, thank you," she expressed, nodding in every direction of the room and making eye contact with as many as she could.

"And before I bid you goodnight, I just have one more thing I'd like to say to you all as a final thank you for coming out tonight to support us in what I anticipate will be an annual event," she said, nodding to Alanna to cue the music. Then, she proceeded to belt out the lyrics to 'Have Yourself a Merry Little Christmas' in the soprano voice she was blessed with. As she sang, Melissa smiled and nodded at people in the audience, deliberately avoiding the front row. When she finished, the audience responded with a standing ovation.

Twenty minutes later, the crowd started to thin out. Some guests retired to the units of the family members they came to support. Others said their goodbyes and left the building, while some grabbed some of the remaining snacks and hung around, listening to the Christmas music playing through the Bluetooth speaker.

"That was quite a surprise performance you gave," the junior Mr. Walker said from behind her as she was moving chairs from one side to the other for easy pick up from the rental company. "I'm even more glad that I decided to come so I could witness it for myself."

"Thank you. I appreciate that," she said, sincerely appreciative of the compliment. "It sounds like you were thinking about not coming. I'm surprised, considering you pretty much insisted your father perform."

"Well, yeah, he wasn't going to let me *not* come. But I had a passing thought that you might not want me here after I behaved so inappropriately, in your opinion." P.J. looked directly into her eyes as he spoke.

Melissa's cheeks burned red at the mention of the incident. She took a deep breath before responding.

"About that. I apologize for jumping to the wrong conclusion about your gesture. The truth of the matter is that I was coming off a rough weekend and was not in the best headspace. I shouldn't have taken it out on you when all you were doing was trying to brighten my day. Regardless of whether it was a professional or personal gesture. It was kind, nonetheless."

His brown eyes brightened. "Oh, so does this mean you're open to it coming from a personal place?"

She shifted from one leg to the other. "Well, was it?" She asked daringly. As much as she had tried not to think about his intention, it had been a recurring thought in the back of her mind.

"And if I say yes, what are you going to do with that revelation?" He quipped.

"I don't know, Mr. Walker. What do you want me to do with it?"

"How about we start with you calling me Paul or P.J. instead of Mr. Walker? That formality is more suited for my father."

"Okay, then, *Paul.* That's easy enough. And I guess you can call me Melissa." She said with a smile.

"Will do, *Melissa,*" He matched her emphasis. "Until the next time I see you. I'm going to bid my father farewell for the night."

"Mmmhmm," Alanna shimmied her way over to Melissa's side the second Paul was out of earshot. "I knew you liked that man. I don't even know why you're giving your mom a hard time."

"Girl, I am not giving her a hard time. I just want her to leave my love life to me."

"Oh, like you left her to hers when you were trying to match her up with every eligible, decent-looking male resident.?" Alanna side-eyed Melissa.

"Well, that's different. My mom has been single far longer than I have. And at this stage of her life, she could use some companionship. I, on the other hand, am not that single. I'm widowed, something that neither you nor she seems to understand."

The word "widow" always stumped Alanna with her comeback. She knew this was a sensitive subject for her friend, and it was never her intent to be hurtful. "Look, boo, I know Maurice will always hold a special place in your heart, but you know he wouldn't want you to be turning down opportunities to let someone love you."

"First of all, nobody is talking love here. Paul Walker Jr. may think I'm kind of cute and might want to take me out on a date, but this is far from a love connection."

"Hmph. Famous last words," Alanna said with a wide grin. "But, real talk, don't make a decision about what it *isn't* without being open to what it could be. BOOM!"

Melissa shot a dramatic eye roll in Alanna's direction as she picked up a coat from the back of a nearby chair and swirled her body into it.

"Do you want me to wait for you so we can leave together?" Alanna asked thoughtfully.

"No, that's okay. I will close out a few things I was working on and then stop by Mom's unit before I leave."

"Okay, be safe and stay warm. I can feel the cold all the way from here." Alanna cautioned as she zipped up her purple puffy coat.

"Alright. I might call you to hang out this weekend."

"Don't call me. Call *Pauuulll.*"

"Girl, BYE!" Melissa shouted as Alanna laughed all the way out the door.

Scene 4

SHE WAS STILL SHAKING her head as she rode the elevator to the third floor. The corridor was practically empty except for a few of the residents who didn't perform. Most of the ones who did perform were wiped from the rising anticipation of the show through showtime. They were likely in their units, showered, and in the bed. She expected as much for her mother but was surprised to find her room empty when she used her spare key to let herself in.

Hmmm, she thought. Before her mother's friend passed away, Melissa would have simply knocked on Ms. Betty's door for her mother. But now that her mother was likely in the company of the senior Mr. Walker, something that Melissa claimed to want for her mother, she thought better of imposing and decided to let the *grown* adults do whatever it is that they were doing. She beelined for her office instead.

She suddenly didn't feel like lingering in her office. After inputting her password, she browsed through her to-do list file on her desktop see what was pressing. Nothing that couldn't wait until Monday, she decided after a few minutes. She signed out of her office management system, closed the browser, and then shut down the computer.

The clock on the dashboard of her car read eight o'clock as Melissa buckled herself in the seatbelt. It's still early for a Friday night, she realized.

Man, when was the last time I went out on a Friday night, she asked herself.

A quick search of her memory bank came back empty. And that was her own doing. Over the last few years, Alanna, being her great best friend, always tried to get her out of the house to do something fun. Melissa declined, opting to sit at home, relax from the work week, and reminisce about Maurice. Their weekends together, before sickness struck, were epic. It is always filled with social gatherings, sampling the latest dining spots around the city, and googobs of cuddle time. Nothing could replace that as far as Melissa had been concerned. After a year of trying, Alanna decided to schedule occasional brunch dates with her, which she knew Melissa would never turn down.

Peanut leaped into her arms the moment she opened the door to her home. Instead of taking her coat off, she grabbed Peanut's leash from the drawer of the table in the hallway and took her outside to do her business. Once back in, she gave her furbaby a treat for holding herself until Melissa came home. While Peanut nibbled on her turkey-flavored treat, Melissa slid out of her coat and boots, put them in the closet, and then went upstairs to change into her favorite thermal pj's.

Returning to the kitchen, she noticed Peanut was finished with her treat.

"Oooh, you must have liked that treat, huh, baby?" She asked, patting Peanut lovingly on the head. "Now it's dinner time." Melissa retrieved her dog food from the pantry, poured it into her bowl, and then took the water dish to the sink for a refill. While Peanut munched on her dinner, Melissa activated the kettle on her counter to heat up water to prepare a cup of Ghirardelli hot chocolate that was gifted to her by the son of one of her residents. With the piping hot chocolate treat, Melissa settled on the couch, placed the mug on the accent table beside her and powered on the TV.

"Hmm, what am I in the mood for?" She asked herself out loud. Right now, nearly every channel is playing something Christmasy. And as Christmas was parallel with romance, she wouldn't even torture herself like that. Another hardship for widows to maneuver during the holiday season. Constant reminders of the love you no longer have in your life.

"Ugh!" She said exasperatingly, turning the television and laying her head back on the couch. Her eyes landed on her and Maurice's wedding picture affixed to the wall in a silver frame. They were so happy and in love. Looking forward to so many years together. They had no way of knowing on that day that time was against them.

Melissa closed her eyes and breathed deeply. Alanna's words were floating around in her head.

Maurice wouldn't want you to close yourself off to love.

"Is that true, honey?" She asked him aloud. "Do you want to give all of this love I have inside of me for you to someone else?"

It won't be the love you have for me. It will be a new and different love. She heard these words in Maurice's voice as clearly as Moses heard the voice of God from the burning bush.

She leaped off the couch, startling Peanut, who had been laying on her foot.

What the... She looked hurriedly from side to side, but she knew there was no one there. At least not physically.

Melissa began to pace the floor, her breathing becoming heavier with each step. *Ohmigod, I'm having a panic attack,* she thought.

She'd never had a panic attack before, so she didn't know what to do. Winging it, she stopped pacing the floor, raised her hands above her head and took slow, deep breaths. A few seconds later her breathing returned to normal, and she decided to ditch the hot chocolate for a glass of wine.

"Come on, Peanut. You get to get another treat since your mom scared the heck out of you while I get something to calm my nerves a bit."

With her glass of wine in hand, she plopped back on the couch, again with Peanut at her foot. Hopefully, there would be no more voices from her dead husband to make her kick the dog again.

Did Maurice really talk to me? She asked herself, taking a sip of sweet red. Melissa was a woman of faith, even though she hadn't been to church in ages. Not even online church which became the popular since the pandemic. But she knew that God was real, and it was likely God speaking to her in the strong memory of her husband's voice. Regardless of whose voice spoke such powerful words, the words had penetrated her to the core.

Yes, Maurice was the love of her life. But if God chose to take him away from her when he did, perhaps God did have another love for her. If her memory served her correctly, a scripture coming to mind said, "*Of all these things I leave with you, the greatest of these is love.*

Love. That thing she wanted so badly for her mother. That thing she had enjoyed so much with Maurice. That thing that was missing from her life right now.

Maybe it is time for me to start enjoying life again, she thought o*utside of work.*

"Alexa," she commanded the little black circular device on her T.V. stand to come to life. "Play my Christmas playlist."

A soulful melody, *I Can Hardly Wait for Christmas,* by the O'jays poured from the speakers. As the guys sang their hearts out for her entertainment, Melissa sipped more red wine. Before the song concluded, she had gone upstairs to her unit to bring down her Christmas tree and decorations. After all, it was a week before Christmas.

Scene 5

THAT WAS AN INTERESTING turn of events, P.J. thought to himself, driving home from the Christmas program at Rose Garden. After scolding him for supposed unprofessionalism and avoiding him over the completion of the stage, Ms. Fields–Melissa had not only apologized to him, she *flirted* with him, too. That was the last thing he expected when he saw her today. No, the *last* thing he expected was her serenade to the audience as a personal thank you for them coming. While the serenade was impressive and spoke volumes, he was slightly more moved by the flirting. It was not only surprising but seemed genuine as well.

No alcohol was served for the occasion, and she didn't seem like the type of woman who would need to swig down some vodka to handle a crowd. She was too much of a professional and a lady for that, at least from what he knew about her. Truthfully, he didn't know much about her, but after their encounter this evening, he wanted to know more. How long had she been married? Why does she still wear a ring? Is she ready to date? Would she prefer a friend?

Hell, the better question is, what do I want? He asked himself.

But what kind of woman was she? He wondered.

He never dated a widow. His experiences had been with never-before-married women or women who had been burned, some literally, by the ex-husbands or boyfriends before him. Whatever the situation, these women always came off as too eager for a good-looking, educated, and financially stable man to improve their lives.

Not Ms. Fields., though. She was disappointed when he showed up in place of his sister the day of his father's move-in, while most women would have been excited to make his acquaintance, P.J. recalled, smiling at the memory.

What is it like to lose a spouse? Had they been happy together when he died? Was the death expected or sudden? Did any of that even matter?

Mmmhmm, I told you son. It's all about the right woman. P.J. recalled words from his father just as another though occurred to him.

Could Melissa be that woman?

Scene 6

MELISSA'S HEART SWELLED with pride as she took in the sight of her work. In an hour, she transformed her home's main floor into a winter wonderland. Snowflakes hung from her ceiling. Red and white beaded garland adorned her fireplace. A quick online shopping and delivery order yielded the four beautiful Poinsettias on her two end tables, dining room, and kitchen tables, atop crisp white tablecloths. A glittery decal was in each window of her house, and her door was a long sheet of snowflake-designed wrapping paper, all setting off a snow-frosted Christmas tree in the corner of the room. It was quite a sight to see, and she felt compelled to share it with her small social media following. She snapped pictures from different angles of the room and created a Facebook post with the caption: *I'm baackk!*

This deserves another glass of wine, she decided. Glass in hand, she returned to the couch, this time with her laptop on her lap and Peanut beside her. Since she had already logged onto Facebook to post her picture, she decided to scroll through the social media platform for the activity she was missing out on. Friend's birthday parties, her high school graduating class was hosting their annual holiday mixer. A former coworker and friend, Angel, had a second child. Another, Cara, had gotten married a few months ago. An event notification indicated that she had been invited. Then there were all the Beyonce *Cuff It* challenge reels.

Everybody is having so much fun, she thought to herself. Judging from all the friend requests, group invites, and event notifications, her friends and associates hadn't forgotten about her. Their lives were moving forward, even after sad and tragic things had happened to them. She was the one living in this isolation, with limited contact with the outside world.

Maybe it's time to change that, she resolved. *Shake things up.*

In the spirit of such, Melissa swallowed the last bit of her wine, moved her cursor to the search bar, and typed, *Paul Walker Jr.*

It was a lot of Paul Walker Jr.'s in the list of results. But as she scrolled through the ones that filled up the length of the screen, the list kept growing. There were several Black, White, biracial, young, and old Pauls and some that had no image at all. Because she hadn't done this for so long, she wasn't annoyed by the process. She grew more anxious with each brown, middle-aged male face that appeared in the tiny boxes.

What was she going to do when she found him? She didn't know. Maybe just check out his profile. See what his marital status was. Observe how he interacted on social media. Maybe click on Messenger and say, "Hi". She would figure that out if she found him.

Finally, after a few minutes of dedicated browsing, she did.

Paul Walker Jr. of One Source Contracting. He was standing in the profile picture. At a worksite, it seemed, giving direction to a couple of workmen. He wore dusty pants and a t-shirt that gave way to a fit upper body.

Seeing that business name almost made her rethink what she was thinking, but she remembered her task: *Shaking things up. Living a little.* Besides, he more than made up for his inconsideration the first time around by building her stage better than she imagined and in time for the Christmas program.

She scrolled his stats: *Single. Christian. Interested in women.*

"Okay, now what?" she said, looking at Peanut, who looked like the sudden noise in the room interrupted her sleep.

Tapping her fingers on the keyboard, Melissa tried to ascertain if he was communicating with someone else on Facebook. Just because of his "single" relationship status didn't mean he wasn't involved in a non-marital kind of way. So, one good time, she looked specifically for pictures of him snuggled up with any woman. Her search came up empty.

You know that doesn't mean anything, her voice of reason said just before a different voice countered with, *Girl, stop it and make your move.*

Without further hesitation, Melissa sent the friend request. A wave of relief washed over her as she closed her laptop, but a notification gave her pause. She pushed it back open and was surprised to see that Paul had accepted her request. Quickly.

That was fast, she thought, sitting at attention. Now she really needed to know what to do! She challenged herself by sending him a friend request and thought it would be the end of her *shaking things up* for the night by stepping out on the wild side. She hadn't expected him to respond so soon. He must have been one of those people always on social media. Well, that was neither here nor there. They were both online right now, and he accepted her request and sent her a message!

Well, good evening, Melissa.

Hello, she typed into the small text box.

So, first, you flirted with me at the center, and now you want to be my social media friend. We've come a long way in a short time, he typed a proverbial mouthful.

That sounded a lot like she was coming across as the chaser in this situation. And even before she married Maurice, she was never in the habit of chasing men. She considered simply ending the conversation, closing her computer, and washing her hands of this mess she had created, but a little bubbly icon appeared at the bottom of the screen, indicating that he was typing. Her interest was piqued.

I'm sorry. You may not know it, but I'm just messing with you. It's funny, I only signed into my account to see if you had a profile I could stalk. You know, to get to know you better without taking the chance of asking you on a date.

Okay, she saw what he did there. She appreciated him expressing his interest in her, which relieved her of the feeling that she had made the first move. A true gentleman.

So, should I sign off and let you stalk my profile? she asked.

Well, you could do that, or, if it's not too late for you to go out, I could pick you up and we can hang out. Grab a bite to eat? A drink or two?

Before Melissa could talk herself out it, she said, "Yes!" and in less than an hour, she was frantically searching her closet.

She couldn't remember the last time she tried to dress cute for a man. In fact, she knew the exact last time.

Three years ago.

For Maurice.

She pushed the thoughts from her past out of her mind as she decided on a pair of skinny jeans, an oversized cowl-neck sweater, and her favorite pair of chocolate brown Ugg boots. The entire time she was getting dressed, she couldn't believe she had agreed to this late, impromptu date with Paul. Was she taking the concept of 'shaking things up' a little too far? Wasn't it enough that she had decorated her house for the first time in three years and then sent a man a friend request on Facebook? All on the same day?

None of the answers to those questions mattered right now. At 10 p.m. her doorbell rang, signaling Paul's arrival.

Right on time, she thought to herself when she heard a knock at her front door. She looked through the peephole, although she knew who was standing on the other side. It's not like anyone else was coming to her house at this time of night.

"Well, hello. I thought you were going to call when you got here," she said with a nervous smile.

"I know I said that, but I'm the kind of man who prefers to pick a woman up from her front door," he said, flashing her a toothy grin."

Melissa returned his smile. "Typically, that's my preference as well, but considering nothing is typical about this evening, I was willing to make an exception." She turned to the hallway closet, about to grab her coat, when he said something else.

"You know, the pictures you posted on your page were great. I was hoping to get an in-person view of these beautiful decorations since I was here. I know it's late now, but I figured it would be too late by the time I bring you back," he said.

"If your goal is to flatter me, it's working," she replied, opening the door for him to step inside. Under normal circumstances, she would not have let a man she barely knows come into her home, but there was nothing normal about this night.

She didn't even know what normal was in the realm of dating. *Shaking things up was in full bloom.*

"Wow!" Paul said when he stepped into her living room. "I've seen some nice Christmas decorations on the outside of people's homes, but inside is something new to me." He explained, taking his time walking past each element of her design, particularly the hanging snowflakes. "I used to think my mother went overboard on the Christmas decorations, but I wish she was still around to decorate until her heart was content."

Sadness resonated in his tone when talking about his mother. Melissa recognized it immediately. She remembered Felicia, Paul's sister, telling her about the passing of her mother and how badly her brother took it. They were extremely close, she explained. Not in a mama's boy kind of way, she added, as though she didn't want Melissa to judge.

"I've always enjoyed holiday decorating. Something I picked up from my mother. But since my husband passed away, I haven't been able to get back into it. Until tonight," she added.

"I'm glad to hear. Thanks for letting me see," he said, walking back toward the door. "Shall we get this party started?"

He took the coat that she held in her hands, motioned for her to turn around, and helped her into it.

"So, my original idea for this night was to find a bar that we could go to, order some appetizers and drinks, hopefully enjoy some nice music and just talk. But seeing how we're both in the spirit of Christmas, I have something else in mind. I know you don't know me very well, but can you trust me to take the lead on this?"

Staying in the spirit of *shaking things up,* she said, "Lead the way," and relaxed into the bucket seat of his Lincoln Navigator and looked at the road ahead. Paul pressed a couple of buttons on the dashboard of the truck until soulful Christmas music was playing through the speakers. They rode silently, enjoying the music, perhaps lost in their thoughts. It wasn't long before he was pulling into the parking lot of the Detroit Zoo. Excitement permeated through her as she knew they could only do one thing at the Detroit Zoo after dark. It was the Wild Lights exhibit.

Paul exited the truck first, walked around to her side and opened the door for her. "We don't have a lot of time. The exhibit is only open for another 30 minutes, but I didn't think we should pass up the opportunity to enjoy it."

"That's okay," Melissa said. "Considering how nippy it is out here, I'm sure we'll be walking fast enough to get through the exhibit in no time. But getting in line for tickets might cut into our time."

"Nope. I purchased the tickets before I got here when the idea first came to me."

"Genius," she said, smiling.

They walked through the entrance and were immediately enthralled by the spectacular lighting display. Every tree along the path they walked was glowing with different color lights.

In between each tree was a different glowing wild animal. Elephants. Giraffes. Polar Bears. Seals. Lions. Tigers. The sight was amazing.

"This is so beautiful. I'm so glad you thought of this." Melissa cooed, smiling from shivering cheek to cheek.

"When I saw the picture you posted, I had a feeling you would enjoy this," he said.

So thoughtful.

"I think my husband would have really enjoyed this." The words slipped out before she could catch them.

Shit. "I'm sorry. I probably shouldn't have said that."

"You don't have to apologize. It's okay. Having memories of your husband is a part of who you are."

"Wow. I really appreciate you saying that. My mom and best friend act like, because it's been three years since he died that I'm supposed to push him out of my head and just move on with life."

"Well, I can't speak for them, but I'm sure their hearts are in the right place. They just want you to be happy again," he responded.

"I know. I want that, too," Melissa said, looking further down the path they were walking. She had to look anywhere but into Paul's eyes. He might have been understanding about her having thoughts of her late husband, but the tears forming in her eyes could give him pause about being on a date with her.

They walked along in comfortable silence until he spoke again. "Do you mind telling me about him?"

That was the last thing she expected to hear from him. Here they were on a date, and he wanted her to talk about her late husband. Sure, it was normal to talk about exes when getting to know someone new. But Maurice wasn't an ex. He died at the height of their love story. She feared that the love she still held for him would permeate her words and Paul would want nothing more to do with her.

"It's okay. I want to hear," he said, sensing her hesitation.

As they completed the short path of the remaining exhibit, she told him the story of herself and Maurice, a shortened version. Either version would have still ended with him passing away before she was ready. There was no sugarcoating that.

She felt like a champagne cork being popped. It had been freeing to talk about Maurice like that. And talking about him and their life together didn't make her any less interested in getting to know Paul Walker Jr., the man she was walking beside in the present. Her only hope was that she didn't spook him, but she didn't know how to ascertain that now.

P.J. had no regrets about asking Melissa about her husband. His curiosity was piqued, but more importantly, he learned something vital during grief therapy after his mother's passing: talking about his mother had significantly aided him in his healing journey. It was a powerful realization, and he understood that while losing a parent and losing a spouse were different magnitudes of loss, the essence of grief remained the same. If openly discussing his loss had been beneficial for him, it might be helpful for her as well. Not that he needed help. But he did want her to consider him a self-space.

By the time she finished sharing her story, P.J. felt confident that he had achieved his objective. The story of Melissa and her husband's relationship, their deep love for each other, flowed from her effortlessly, like warm, melted butter. Her voice was gentle and steady, showing no signs of an emotional struggle or the need to hold back tears. Here was a woman who deeply loved her husband and perhaps was still grappling with the unfairness of his premature departure. It led P.J. to speculate if this lingering love was the reason she still wore her wedding ring. He couldn't be certain, and he concluded that tonight was not the right time to ask that that question.

"Thank you for sharing that with me. I'm sorry you lost him so soon into your marriage," he said when she became quiet.

"Thank you for asking me."

They had made it to his truck. He opened the passenger door, took her hand into his, and helped her inside. When he climbed in on the other side, he checked the clock on the dashboard. 10:51 pm.

"I wish we had more time for the festival of lights in Wayne, Michigan, but they close at eleven. If you're not in a rush to go home, I'd like to take you somewhere else."

"Sure," Melissa said. "And on the way, you can tell me something about yourself that you'd like me to know."

"Sounds like a plan," he said, starting the truck and then shifting it into drive. The sounds of a soulful Christmas returned through the stereo system, but Paul turned the volume down so Melissa could hear him speak.

"So, what would you like to know?" He asked.

Melissa tilted her head, considering what she wanted to know. She could be typical and ask him about his past relationships. Especially about the fact that he had never been married. But she opted for something else that she wanted to know.

"Why did you decide to go into business for yourself?" She could have guessed based on her own "why," but everybody's reason was different.

P.J.'s face radiated a brightness that rivaled the luminous displays they had just witnessed at the light festival as he began answering her question. He spoke about his passion for working with his hands and the joy of bringing a client's vision to fruition. His enthusiasm was palpable as he detailed the transformative process of turning ideas into tangible realities. However, it was not until he delved into the subject of his mentoring program for inner-city kids that Melissa had a profound realization. As he spoke about his ambitions for these kids, about what he hoped they would learn and achieve by the time they completed his program, Melissa understood something significant. In that moment, she recognized the depth of his character. It dawned on her that she could, quite possibly, fall in love with a man like this.

Their date ended just before midnight with Melissa feeling like she was walking on air. Clearly, Paul enjoyed it, too, because she awoke the next morning to a sweet text message:

Good morning Melissa. Thank you for spending time with me yesterday,

Opening up about yourself and your late husband and letting me do the

same about my life. It was refreshing and warm, though it was cold

as hell outside :) I hope to see you soon.

P.J

That message led to a string of text messages between them over the next two days. He was finishing up a job that Saturday and watching football on Sunday with some friends. But the messages were enough to keep her giddy as she shopped online, relaxed on the couch with Peanut, watching the second season of the wildly popular Netflix series *Bridgerton.*

Act 3

Scene 1

MONDAY MORNING, P.J. awoke with a smile on his face, and he knew it was all because of the weekend he had with Melissa. He couldn't believe how much fun he had with her. Not just on their date Friday night but the text conversation over the weekend. After Saturday, it had taken everything for him not to cancel football with the fellas and invite to breakfast, lunch, or dinner with him. But he didn't want to move too fast. For very different reasons, this was something neither of them had done in quite some time. As for himself, he didn't want to make mistakes that he had in the past. He really wanted to get to know this woman and let her really get to know him.

In the past, he had often been labeled as a workaholic, criticized for taking breaks only when it suited his schedule. This perception, however, didn't fully capture the reality. The truth lay in the fact that he had yet to encounter a woman who sparked in him a desire to prioritize anything over his business endeavors. His previous partners had often expected him to invest his hard-earned income in extravagant activities like dinner dates, concerts, and vacations. They would then voice their dissatisfaction when his work commitments, which often extended beyond standard business hours, interfered with their plans. Melissa, on the other hand, as a fellow business owner, might possess the understanding and appreciation for the dedication required to sustain a successful business.

P.J., got up from his bed and made his way to the kitchen. He opened the freezer and retrieved a breakfast sandwich, placing it in the microwave. He set the timer for three and a half minutes, following the package instructions. While waiting, he headed to his home office to start up his computer. Once it was booted, he logged into his email, scanning for any new appointment requests. During his routine check, a Google alert caught his eye – a recent review of his company. He always eagerly anticipated reading these updates.

He clicked the link and immediately noticed it was from Rose Garden Senior Living. Then he noticed the one star.

What the hell?

He read it. Then he read it again. And then he read it one more time, angrier each time. First of all, what the hell was she talking about with this missed appointment? He jumped to his calendar, searching for the date in question. *Nothing.* That day he was moving his father in at Rose Garden. He remembered it clearly. There was one appointment that he had, and he called the client a week prior to reschedule. The client was more than understanding and appreciative of the call. That was the kind of business owner that he was. A responsible one. That's why he had never received anything less than a five-star review.

P.J. was livid! The microwave was beeping away in the kitchen, but his appetite was lost. He could not believe the audacity of this woman to have ripped his company to shreds online and then went on a damn date with him like she had nothing of the kind. Here, he was thinking that as a business owner, she would be different, but it turns out she was like the rest of them. Maybe one of the worst. A wolf in sheep's clothing.

Scene 2

MELISSA SPENT THE MORNING onboarding the new administrative assistant, Mya, that she hired. Between checking on Mya and her regular Monday meetings with the state health department, it was noon before she realized that she hadn't heard from Paul all morning. Not that he was obligated to reach out to her, but she thought he would after the weekend they just had. But he could have gotten busy with work just like she did. Since things had slowed down, she reached for her phone and texted him.

Hi, Paul. I hope your Monday is going well. I look forward to hearing

from you soon.
Melissa

THE REST OF HER AFTERNOON was clear, so she visited her mother's unit. *If* her mother was even there. Melissa didn't know the extent of her mother's involvement with the senior Mr. Walker, but the irony was not lost on her that both of them had spent Friday night, at least, with the Walker men. She wasn't sure if she was going to mention it to her mother yet. It was still very early with what was going on between her and Paul Jr. She definitely liked him, and he seemed to like her. But that didn't mean that they were relationship-bound. And she couldn't even say that she was ready for that. A relationship. But a friendship that could *become* a relationship. She was ready for that.

Her mother was in her room when she arrived. Lorraine was wearing a beige sweater and loose-fitting jeans.

"Hello, daughter. Come on in," she said chipperly.

"Hey, Mom. This isn't your usual bum-around-the-facility outfit. Going somewhere?" Melissa asked.

"As a matter of fact, I am. Felicia, you know, Paul's daughter?" She asked.

"Yes, I remember. I finally met her Friday."

"Mmmhmm, yes. Well, she has an extra ticket for the Lions game because, I guess, Paul Jr. can't go, and Paul asked me if I wanted to go, and I said yes."

"Oh," Melissa said, immediately wondering why Paul wasn't going. Maybe something happened at work, after all, and that's why he hasn't reached out or responded to her text message. She hoped everything was okay. "Well, you look nice. I'm sure you'll enjoy the game."

"Well, you know I will, but I won't enjoy it as much as I enjoyed our Christmas program. That was so much fun, and I'm so proud of you for putting that together!"

"Aww, thank you, Mom. But I couldn't have done anything without all of you."

"Yes, well, it started with you and ended with you too, with that performance you gave at the end," Lorraine crooned.

"And I think Paul Jr. was just as impressed as everyone else was. Was he telling you that when you two were in the back corner whispering to each other?"

"Mom! We weren't in any back corner. But, yes, he did compliment me on the program as well as my performance." Melissa's cheek reddened, realizing that they'd had an audience.

"Mmmhmm. I bet he did. Y'all seemed to be hitting it off. Finally."

You don't know how much, she thought to herself. "We had a nice conversation," was all Melissa said on that matter. "Okay, Mom. Have a good time. Let me know when you get back."

"Yes, Mom," Lorraine replied sarcastically.

Back in her office, Melissa started a text to Paul.

Hi Paul. I hope everything is okay. I heard about your canceling

with your family. Call or text when you get a chance.

BUT SHE DIDN'T SEND it. An underlying feeling in her gut said the text was overkill. She'd already texted him first today. Her day had been busy, too, but she still found a moment to reach out. And, obviously, if he could take a moment to cancel with his sister, whether by text or phone call, he could have at least shot her a "hello" message. Of course, she wasn't on the same level as his family, but she thought he liked her enough not to be blowing her off like this. It may have been a while since she was out with a man, but she still had a standard for how she expected to be treated. And this wasn't it.

Melissa deleted the text that she typed to Paul and scrolled to the ongoing message thread between her and Alanna. She needed some girlfriend time.

Hey lady. Can you meet for dinner after work today? You pick the place.

At six o'clock, Melissa was sitting across from Alanna at Cooper's Hawk Restaurant & Winery in Troy. It was a little further than Melissa preferred to drive on a weekday, but she really needed to talk to Alanna about this Paul thing. Over two glasses of Riesling and house bread, Melissa filled her in on her and Paul's date Friday night and the following two days.

"Wait! Are you freaking kidding me?" Alanna asked wide-eyed. "I mean, when I left you on Friday night, you were acting so blasé about him, and now you're telling me that you hit him up on Facebook and went out on a date! I can't believe you're just now telling me this."

Melissa expected this reaction, so she let her friend feel and express her feelings. But she would only let her do it for a few minutes. She needed to get the other part of the story. The part that was perplexing her.

When Alanna stuffed another piece of bread in her mouth, Melissa continued with the events of today and, at the end, asked, "What is up with that?"

"Girl, if I had these men figured out, I would be married by now or, at least, in a successful relationship."

"Well, friend, that's why I'm asking. I figure you've been dealing with these frivolous games that men play long enough to decipher this for me."

"In that case, my expert opinion is that he's full of shi...." Alanna was interrupted by a young Black man with shoulder-length locs appearing at their table to take their order. They both ordered the house pasta with Brussels sprouts and were alone at the table again.

"I swear I don't get it. First, God takes the love of my life. And, then, when I finally take the chance on a guy who I think is a decent, he ghosts me after showing me such a lovely night out and making me feel special the whole weekend. That was my first time since Maurice died, not sulking the weekend away."

Alanna's face formed a frown. "I knew that's what you've been doing. That's why I've been trying to get your butt out of the house!"

"I know. I know. I just had to do it my way until it was time for something different. And I thought Paul *was* that something different. I can't believe I was *so* wrong about him."

"Okay, look. Before you write him completely off, give him the benefit of the doubt. Especially considering that he did cancel the game with his family. I know our Lions aren't always the winning team, but real fans still look forward to watching them play. Maybe something important came up." Alanna said rationally.

"But why hasn't he texted me back? Why couldn't he just tell me that?"

"Okay. Let me tell you something I have learned about men over my dating years," Alanna looked at her pointedly. "They are a lot slower than women are about feeling any obligations to communicating things they may feel are private. You see, we give too much too soon. They make us prove that we are worthy of intimate details of their life. So just keep that in mind when considering what he *should* be telling you."

"Okay. I get that, but he still didn't respond to the message I sent him."

Alanna shrugged. "Hey, nobody said dating is easy. I wish this didn't happen to you on your first time out the gate. Only God, and maybe your mother, knows how much I want to see you dating and enjoying life again. Don't let this first bump in the road make you put the bike back in the garage."

"Really?" Melissa asked speculatively. "A bike analogy? That's all you got for me, huh?"

"Pretty much! Welcome back to the world of dating!" They clinked their glasses together and signaled to the waiter for another round.

Scene 3

BY THE TIME CHRISTMAS Eve arrived, Melissa yearned to erase the entire episode involving Paul from her memory. She wished to forget that it was he who had assisted with moving his father into the Rose Garden. She wanted to obliterate the memory of him being the one who had constructed the stage in her recreation room. Most of all, she struggled with the reality that he was the son of the man her mother was increasingly becoming fond of day by day. Yet, despite her efforts, she couldn't.

Each day, as she walked past the stage, glimpses of him flashed through her mind. Seeing his father, either in the company of her mother or by himself, invariably brought his image to the forefront. The sound of Christmas music, which now seemed omnipresent in the office, transported her back to the time she listened to it with him in his truck during their date. Her phone, too, served as a constant reminder of their weekend conversation and, more poignantly, the fact that he had not reached out to her since. While she wanted to harbor anger towards him, disappointment was the predominant emotion she felt - disappointed that she let herself feel giddy again.

Melissa was glad that she didn't tell her mother about what happened. She didn't need her mother pestering her about the situation. Or even worse, involving Paul Sr. She and Paul Jr. were adults, even if only one of them were acting like it.

With no one at work having a clue about the potential romance that sparked in one moment and died in the next, Melissa could comfortably walk the corridor of Rose Garden, wishing people a Merry Christmas without anyone being the wiser of the additional weight she was carrying. First, the usual of missing Maurice, and now, being made a fool of by Paul.

Luckily, today, there was hardly anyone to see. Most residents were in their units with visiting family members or off-site with family or friends. Melissa had come in to drop off fresh baked goods to those she knew were celebrating alone. She was also picking her mother up to spend the night and Christmas day with her. In the last few years, Melissa celebrated with her mother at Rose Garden because she hadn't been decorating her home for the holidays as expected. But since she did this past weekend, she was looking forward to her mother seeing what she had done.

She knocked on her mother's door, and Lorraine opened the door with her overnight bag in her hand.

"I'm ready," she announced as though it weren't obvious. "Now you know we have to stop by the grocery store because I know you don't have everything I need for dinner."

At the store, Melissa noticed her mother was putting more in the basket than was necessary for the two of them.

"Mom, why so much? You know neither of us is going to eat that much." Melissa said.

"Oh, I forgot to tell you that I invited Paul and his son over for dinner. Paul's daughter and her family..." Her mother was explaining, but Melissa couldn't hear anything else.

This could not be for real, she was thinking. Now, she immediately regretted not telling her mother about what happened with her and Paul. If she had known, there was no way she would have invited him to Melissa's home. But Paul knew. So maybe he would do the right thing and decline the invitation. Considering he never responded to her message and had not initiated any further contact with her, he obviously didn't want to see her again.

"Did you hear what I said?" Her mother was asking, snapping her out of her thoughts.

"Uhh, no. I'm sorry. What were you saying?"

"I said I'm going to take care of all the cooking, so you don't have to worry about anything. Okay?"

"Okay," Melissa lied because she had very much to worry about.

Scene 4

PAUL WAS NOT VIOLENT by any means, but if he could put his hands on his sister right now, he would. She didn't even *like* her in-laws. Why did she have to choose now of all times to have dinner with them? Because of her, he had to be the one to accompany his father to dinner with Ms. Lorraine at Melissa's house. Paul's only way out was to tell his father about his relationship with Melissa and what he discovered about her later. He dreaded hearing his father go on about him using Melissa's online review of his business as an excuse. His father, not being a business owner, couldn't understand Paul's feelings about his business. As a business owner, Melissa understood, which is why her review hit him so hard. It wasn't just the review itself, but also that she didn't take it down after he built her an even better stage than she'd asked for.

It was a rare occasion that he had to come face to face with a woman he kicked to the curb. It was easy to ignore her messages at the height of his anger. A couple of days later, when he remembered her smile as they walked through the light display, his heart softened a bit. He had decided to stay away from her a little longer to keep those feelings at bay. How was that going to work if he had to show up for Christmas dinner at her house?

Scene 5

IT HAD BEEN TOO LONG since Melissa awoke to her mother's cooking on a holiday or any other day that she could remember. Sadly, she couldn't enjoy it because of the circumstances. In less than four hours, she was going to be face to face with Paul, the first man she had cracked the door to her heart for since Maurice died and the first man to ghost her.

He had a lot of nerve to be coming to her house after ghosting her. What kind of man has *that* kind of nerve? An arrogant one, she presumed. She had obviously misjudged his character. What she had originally thought was unprofessional turned out to be much worse. He was cruel.

At 3pm, she stepped out of her room, dressed in a pair of sleek black faux leather pants paired with a striking off-the-shoulder, solid red sweater. Determined to make a strong impression, she had meticulously chosen her outfit with the knowledge that the man who had wronged her was on his way to her house. She was resolute in ensuring she looked her absolute best upon his arrival.

"Wow!" Her mother said when she entered the kitchen. "Don't you look great?"

"Thanks, Mom. Dinner smells delicious."

"Thank you. You'll be cooking like this again once you let a man into your heart again."

"Sure, Mom." *I tried Mom,* she longed to say but didn't. Instead, she started setting the dining room table.

The Walker men arrived promptly at 4 pm. Both were impeccably dressed. Paul Sr. in black dress pants, grey shirt, black tie, and black suit jacket. Paul Jr. wore faded jeans, a blue shirt, and a brown suede sport coat. *Handsome as ever,* Melissa thought begrudgingly.

"Merry Christmas!" She said merrily, opening the door wide to usher them inside.

"Merry Christmas," the men said, not quite simultaneously. Melissa and Paul avoided eye contact while Paul Sr. and her mom vividly expressed their mutual joy being in each other's company again.

Lorraine spared no effort in preparing an exquisite dinner. The menu featured perfectly baked lamb chops, alongside a rich and creamy macaroni and cheese. Complementing these were sweet, tender candied yams and collard greens. To round off the meal, she included freshly baked yeast dinner rolls, adding a comforting touch to the lavish spread. Dinner was served family style. Lorraine and Paul Sr. chatted amongst themselves until one of them realized that neither Melissa nor Paul Jr were not engaged in a conversation of their own.

"You two are awfully quiet," Lorraine noted first. "I didn't expect that after how chatty you all were after the Christmas program."

"Yeah, that's right," Paul Sr. chimed in, sending both Melissa and Paul Jr. in bubbling messes.

"Oh well, that was...," Melissa began first, shifting uncomfortably in her chair.

"Uhh, well, it was..." Paul stammered in.

"Look, how about you two make yourselves useful since you have nothing to say. Y'all can start cleaning the table off and bring out the desserts."

"I can take care of it myself, Mom. *He* can stay right where he is." Melissa said saucily. She hoped that her mother and Paul Sr. were too caught up in each other to have noticed the annoyance in her tone. But she did *not* want Paul Walker Jr. feeling any more comfortable in her home than he obviously felt to have even show up today, considering how he treated her.

She stood up, started with her own plate, and was about to pick up Paul's when he suddenly stood. "I can get my own, thank you."

Their parents resumed their conversations like nothing was happening all around them. Melissa's hands were planted firmly on her hips in the kitchen when Paul entered right behind her.

"You know, you, nor your attitude are welcome in my home. My mother may have invited you by way of your father, but I did not invite you here. And I don't need or want you walking through my house as though I welcomed you here."

"Hey, I didn't want to be here anymore than you want me here. I came here for my father and *your* mother." Paul said in a hushed but stern voice.

"I don't care why you're here, but I don't want you in my kitchen. You can go sit back down at the table with *your* father and *my* mother!"

"I don't know how you used to talk to your husband, but ..." Paul began, but caught himself but not soon enough.

"Excuse me!"

"I'm sorry. I didn't mean that." Paul's tone was softer but still angry.

"Oh sure, I'm sure you didn't mean that like you didn't mean to ghost me after pretending to be a decent guy."

"Whatever. I'm not the one who was pretending. That was you."

"What? What are you talking about?" she asked, confused.

"I'm talking about you slamming my business and then going on a date with me like everything was all good."

"Slamming your business? What are you talking about?" She asked again, but the memory hit her like a train. "Ohh, you mean..."

"Hmph, coming back to you now?"

"Actually, it is, but..."

"It ain't no buts about it. You slammed me for missing an appointment that wasn't on my calendar in the first place. Then, when I completed the job, beyond your expectations, I see you didn't go back to the site to mention that. As a business owner yourself, a black business owner at that, you should be just as quick to compliment another black business owner as you were to tear it down."

Paul picked up the red velvet cake in the clear cake dish and walked back to the dining room, leaving a dumbfounded Melissa in the middle of her kitchen.

It was annoyingly cute and irritating that Melissa and Paul's parents were so captivated by each other that neither of them noticed the tension between their children. On the ride back to the Rose Garden, Lorraine only talked about how good dinner was with the Walker men.

"You know you and P.J. should have talked more to each other. Y'all might find that you have a lot in common. Wouldn't that be a hoot? A mother and daughter dating a father and son," She giggled like a schoolgirl while Melissa stewed in anger.

After dropping her mother off at the center, Melissa rushed home to log on to her computer and locate the Google review of Paul's company.

Okay, she admitted, it wasn't a good review. But then, aren't bad reviews meant to be just that—bad? From where she stood, he simply hadn't shown up as expected. She had every right to be upset. Frankly, if she had known it was One Source Contracting recommended by Paul's father, she wouldn't have hired them. Then again, if she hadn't, she also wouldn't have gotten the stage in time for her event.

If P.J. had seen her review sooner, he likely would not have suggested his father as a performer. Then that would have caused him not to be there on performance day. And, then that would have led to the two of them not having any conversation that night.

No conversation.

No friend request.

No date.

She sank into her couch as a truth occurred to her that she didn't want to acknowledge. Once the stage was complete, she should have gone back to the site and given a favorable review. Contrary to what he thought of her, she was a person who gave favorable reviews to companies that did good work for her, especially to other black businesses. This was an oversight.

A big one, obviously.

"It's like he didn't even give me the benefit of the doubt before he drew the worst conclusion," Melissa was saying to Alanna over the phone after she left her mother in her unit at the Garden.

"Yeah, but in all fairness, you didn't give him the benefit of the doubt when he missed the appointment. And you knew he was at your place, moving his father in. That's an understandable reason to have forgotten a consultation appointment."

She hated it when her friend called her to the carpet. "Actually, I didn't know that part that until much later.

"Still," Alanna persisted. "I know you've been frustrated with these contractors since the pandemic. But you know how things are for that industry right now, and you have a thing with not cutting people any slack."

"Really, Lana? How about you cut me some slack?"

"Hmm, let's just move on to how you're going to make this right."

"Make it right? The man ghosted *me*. I know you don't think I'm supposed to chase him."

"Not chase him, but at least apologize. That will at least put the ball back in his court. I can tell that you really like him. We wouldn't even be having this conversation if you didn't."

"I liked him until he ghosted me," Melissa huffed.

Alanna ignored Melissa's last comment. "Just apologize."

Their conversation ended a short time later, but Melissa spent the rest of the night wondering how she could apologize to someone so angry with her. It might have been easier to let the whole thing go. After all, they'd only had *one* date. That shouldn't be so hard to forget.

Scene 6

BY THE TIME NEW YEAR'S Eve arrived, forgetting about Paul and their date proved harder than Melissa could have imagined. Not only did Christmas music and lights at night bring thoughts of him to her mind, but so did seeing his father with her mother every day that she went to work. They were equally adorable and annoying.

There wasn't much work for Melissa to do in the office. And with her mom occupied with Paul Sr., Melissa couldn't use her as a reason to hang around. So, she was home for the next couple of days with only incessant thoughts of Paul and regret to keep her company.

She was miserable. This was worse than mourning the life she lost with Maurice. She was used to the hurt. That had become as normal as breathing for her. But this hurt her in a way that she didn't want to get comfortable with.

But what could she do to change it?

Apologize. The advice from Alanna.

What would an apology accomplish? Make him forgive her? Resolve her of her guilt? She wondered if it would crack the door he had slammed shut after reading that review. She wouldn't know unless she tried.

How does one apologize to a man? she thought. She wasn't used to being on this end of apologies. Nor could she recall a man being as angry at her as P.J. was.

Would he prefer a more direct approach, like a phone call? Or would a text suffice?

She preferred a text. That way, if he laughed at her efforts, she wouldn't have to see it up close and personal.

Before reaching out to him directly, she needed to do something else. She signed into Google and searched for his business name. Once it was on the screen, she posted a glowing review, including pictures of the stage he built. That was a start.

It was 6 pm. She lifted herself from the couch and walked into the kitchen. She could use a glass of wine while she worked on the next step of her apology.

Scene 7

P.J. WAS TRYING TO enjoy himself at his friend Rick's house. Rick and his wife, Veronica, always hosted the best NYE party with a live DJ, karaoke, and catered food. And plenty of Veronica's single friends were in attendance. In years past, he reveled in the attention. But tonight, his head wasn't in it. As upset as he had been with Melissa, she was still on his mind. Specifically, the connection he felt between them on their date. He couldn't call it love, but it was something different than he had experienced with a woman in a long time. His interest had been piqued for what could come next.

Then he saw that damn review.

Brian didn't think it was that big of a deal. "I agree that she should have given another review when we finished, but her first review was based on her first experience."

"You can be so understanding because it's not your business," P.J. shot back.

"True, but if you like the woman, I think it's something y'all could talk about as two business owners. Client and contractor. Misunderstandings happen."

P.J. didn't appreciate Brian's rationale that day. But after a few days, specifically after seeing her and arguing with her on Christmas day, his anger began to subside. Especially times like now. The vision of her standing in the middle of her kitchen, hands planted on her hips came to mind. If she had the physical strength to throw him out, she would have done it.

Then there was a vision of the reluctant smile that lurked behind her eyes throughout their date. They were truly enjoying their unexpected time together. He wished he could have turned back the hands of time before he saw that review. Calling her was at the top of his agenda that day. But he'd opened his email first.

Damn, he thought whenever it came to mind. There was a misconception among Black Americans that it was so easy for a Black man to find a good Black woman. He could attest to the falsehood of that. This was a case in point. Melissa started out so well, then *blam! Sucker punch to the gut.*

A notification to his phone interrupted his thoughts. He swiped up to see what it was. His "Ring" camera was had notified him of motion at his door. By the time the app opened to the camera, the person was gone but he could see the shadow of an object on the porch.

Interesting.

He hadn't ordered anything recently and wasn't expecting any belated Christmas gifts. This wasn't a pressing matter, but he decided to use it as an excuse to leave. He was feeling like a buzz kill as everyone else around him was smiling, laughing, and enjoying each other's company.

He lifted himself from the couch and went in search of Rick. He found him in the bar of the basement making the signature cocktail for the occasion.

"Hey, man. I'm going to cut get of here. There's a package at my door, and I don't want it to be out front all night."

"Come on now, bro. You know ain't nobody going on your porch tonight," Rick said, calling him out. "What's the real deal?

"I'm just not in a partying mood tonight, but I really do have a package that just got delivered. This party is great, but I'm more excited to go home and see what this package is if that's any indicator of how I'm feeling tonight."

"Alright, bro. Do you, man, and Happy New Year."

Paul expected more of a fight from Rick, but he was glad he didn't give him one today. He just wanted to get out of there. It was 9:30 pm. Leaving now, he'd be home by 10. With light traffic on the streets, he made it by 9:50.

He opened the garage with the remote inside the truck and drove inside. After taking his coat off and hanging it inside the closet, he walked through the house until he reached the front door. He opened it and was surprised to see an Edible Arrangement of strawberries, pineapples, and cantaloupe chunks.

This was the last thing he was expecting. He knew from experience that Edible Arrangements didn't deliver after 5 pm, and this arrived on his porch well after seven. Whoever delivered this did so personally. And they went through the trouble of avoiding the camera so the arrangement would actually be a surprise.

Paul brought the package in, sat it on his kitchen table, and looked for the card.

Paul,

Please accept my apology for the review. You did a great job for me

on short notice, and you're right; I should have posted that, too.

I likely would have if I hadn't gotten so distracted by the owner of

the business, himself. I like you, Paul. I want to see you again. If

you're up for it, come outside to your driveway.

Melissa

My driveway? Was she serious? Paul darted toward the front room of his house to look out the windows. Sure enough, bright headlights were beaming through.

What is wrong with this woman? What is she thinking? How did she even know where he lived?

Of all the questions running through his mind, he was ignoring the ones that mattered: *Was he up for it? Did he want to see her again?*

That was an easy yes. But this was in direct conflict with his stubborn gene. He was angry with her. Intentionally or not, she went after the one thing he cherished more than anything–his business. He only loved his family more, but he did *like* her. *A lot.* Maybe that counted for something.

He looked out the window, wanting to see through the darkened window. He wondered what she was wearing. How was her hair styled? Was she wearing lip gloss? Perfume? The only way to find that out was to take his stubborn self out to her car.

Paul opened his front door and walked in search of the answers he wanted and whatever else she had for him.

Ohmigod! Ohmigod! Ohmigod! Melissa's heart started beating a mile a minute when she saw his front door open. It had taken so long since she watched him take the bouquet into his house, she'd almost given up on him. But now that he was walking toward her car, she was freaking out!

Breathe, sis. Breathe. Her heart was beating like an out-of-control wildfire.

Paul arrived at her car window. She pressed the button to roll the window down.

"Hi," she uttered, her voice tinged with hesitation. She compelled herself to maintain eye contact. She hadn't driven all the way here tonight to shy away. Just a couple of hours earlier, while seated on her couch, she had resolved to confront the chaos she felt responsible for creating. Reflecting on the profound sadness that had engulfed her in recent years, she realized she wasn't honoring the memory of her husband or the love they shared. She recognized that she was allowing life –her life—to pass her by. Maurice would not want that for her.

As unprofessional as she originally thought it was for Paul to have sent that Edible Arrangement to her office, the truth was that she liked the tingle of excitement when she saw it. On their date, she enjoyed the quiet chemistry brewing between them. She wanted more of that, and she wanted it with Paul.

"Hello," he replied.

"Are you going to get in or just stand outside making me cold with this window down?"

"Is there a destination in mind?" he asked.

"I guess you'll have to get in and see," she retorted. He relented, walking around to the passenger seat and climbing inside. "Do you trust me?" She asked.

"Can I?" he quipped.

"Something else you're going to have to find out." She turned the volume on the music as she watched him put on his seat belt. A few minutes later, the smile she was expecting began to curl on his lips.

"Oh, okay, you must know this is my favorite female artist of all time," he said, as the smooth sounds of Sade filled the space around them.

"Yes, I do," she declared with a sense of triumph. Having posted her follow-up review on Google, she swiftly navigated to Facebook to scrutinize his profile. There, she meticulously noted his favorite singers, movies, foods, and hobbies, and planned her actions accordingly. She was fully prepared, with an array of additional surprises in store for him.

Melissa followed the instructions of her GPS and let Paul relax into the music for fifteen minutes of the twenty-minute ride to their destination.

"Do you mind taking the box out of the glove box for me?" She asked.

"Sure. No problem," he said. With a quick squeeze of the lever, he opened the compartment door. At first, he only saw the car manual. Then, with a second look, he noticed a box on top of the manual.

"He pulled the box out and asked her, "Do you need me to take something out of here?"

"Yes, please. Help yourself," she said, smiling.

"To what?" He asked, visibility confused.

"To what's in the box, silly."

He slowly opened the box and threw his head back against the headrest. "Stop it! Cigars? You bought me some cigars?"

"I did."

"Wow! What are you up to?" he asked, speculatively?

"Just showing you a good time like you did me on Christmas Eve. Are you okay with a woman doing something nice for you?"

A smirk slipped from his lips. "I'm okay with it. Just not used to it. You know most women are all about what men do for them."

"Well, maybe you haven't met the right woman."

"You might be right," he said, lighting the cigar with the lighter she included in the box. "Do you partake?" He asked, indicating the cigar.

"No, I've never even thought about smoking a cigar. Smoking of any kind, really."

"Look at you. A selfless woman if I ever met one," Paul smiled and took a puff of his cigar.

Melissa's chest swelled with pride at the joy across his face. It felt good to bring joy to another person besides the residences of Rose Garden.

She took exit I75 South. She had wanted to take him to the Wayne County Light Festival, but they closed at 11 pm. So, they were going to a place that never shut down. Downtown Detroit. And this time of the year, it was the most beautiful.

"Well, this is nice, but is all of this supposed to make up for your review of my business?"

"Not exactly," she said somberly. "I owe you an apology. Not so much for the negative review because that was my genuine and first experience with your company," she began. He was about to object, but she hushed him with a palm-facing hand. "But you were right. I should have retracted the review or at least follow it up with my favorable review of the great work you did for me. You should also know that I have since done that."

"You did?"

"Yes. But tonight is about more than making things right about that. It is about picking up where we left off," she said, boldly taking her hand from the steering wheel and placing it on top of his. "It is about seeing if you are as willing as I am to leave the past in the past and look forward to what could be a bright future if it's meant to be."

Paul flipped his hand in hers so that their fingers could intertwine into each other's. The palm of his hand was as warm as the feeling in her heart when he responded favorably.

"Let's do it."

Melissa and Paul's hands remained intertwined as she drove them through the remainder of the path of holiday lights. The sweet, soulful sounds of Sade's *Cherish the Day* played through the speaker. She took the long way back to his house so that they were closing out one year together and beginning the new one the same.

Don't miss out!

Visit the website below and you can sign up to receive emails whenever LaCharmine (L.A.) Jefferson publishes a new book. There's no charge and no obligation.

https://books2read.com/r/B-A-AWBCB-FKCSC

Connecting independent readers to independent writers.

About the Author

LaCharmine (L.A) Jefferson is an author of contemporary women's fiction novels, Unfinished Business and Reconciliation to Hell. Her creative nonfiction has appeared in two anthologies: Daddy: Reflections of Father-Daughter Relationships, A Widow's Resilience, and more recently, Chicken Soup for the Soul: I'm Speaking Now. L.A. blogs about her writing journey and is a co-host of the podcast, Conversations Between Widows. L.A. is a mother of two adult children and grandmother of two adorable girls.

Read more at https://lajefferson.com.